Blue Moon Dragon

A Steamy Shifter Romance

Shelley Munro

Munro Press

Blue Moon Dragon

Print ISBN: 978-1-99-106354-0
Digital ISBN: 978-0-473-34029-2

Editor: Mary Moran

Cover: Kim Killion, The Killion Group, Inc.

Munro Press, New Zealand.

First Munro Press electronic publication March 2015

First Munro Press print publication June 2024

DEDICATION

For Paul, my husband, partner in crime, and fellow adventurer.
Every day is a good day.

Introduction

Take a walk on the dragon side...

On her 25th birthday, Emma Montrose decides it's time to show bad boy investigator Jack Sullivan that she's more than an efficient secretary. She's a woman with needs, and she *wants* him.

Jack is a taniwha, a dragon shifter, who requires women to satiate the demands of the beast within. Casual, and nothing more is his operating procedure. Voluptuous Emma has relationship written all over her, and Jack intends to keep far, far away, especially during the coming blue moon, which will erode his restraint.

Then, his job forces the reluctant Jack and ecstatic Emma undercover as a couple. Thrown together at a luxury resort to investigate a drugs case, pretense and reality blur generating hot lovin' laced with risk...

Pronunciation Guide and Glossary

Taniwha – a dragon from Māori mythology. Some—water dragons—live in lakes, rivers or the sea. Legend says a taniwha lives at every bend of a river. Other taniwhas are cave dwellers and have the ability to fly. Some are benevolent while others are mischievous tricksters or true villains. Taniwha is pronounced tun-ee-far.

Hone – Māori for John, and a very common Christian name. Hone is pronounced Hon-ee.

Pikelet – a bite-size pancake, which is often eaten for morning or afternoon tea in New Zealand and also Australia. I like mine with raspberry jam and whipped cream.

Hokey Pokey Ice cream – vanilla ice cream filled with lumps of honeycomb.

Morepork – a native New Zealand owl. The European settlers thought the bird's cry sounded as if it were demanding "more pork" and the name stuck.

Netball – a popular sport played mainly by women in New Zealand, Australia, United Kingdom, South Africa, and Jamaica. Two teams of seven players attempt to score the most goals during a game. The goal is similar to a basketball goal but it does not have a backboard. The ball is passed from player to player rather than bounced as in basketball. I used to play netball and held a defense position due to my height.

CHAPTER 1

"Good morning, George Taniwha Investigators and Security." Emma forced a bright smile and hoped her despondency didn't crawl down the telephone line. Twenty-five years old today.

Twenty-five!

And she still hadn't plucked up the courage to approach Jack Sullivan and ask him out on a date—despite this being the age of equal opportunity. The male in question sauntered past her desk and strode into George Taniwha's office without giving her a second glance.

A man to die for...

Emma sighed and stared at the bronze nameplate on the door in frustration. So, she wasn't the most beautiful woman in New

Zealand. She was built with the word generous in mind. A large arse and a chest made to house her big heart. Or at least that was what her high school boyfriend had informed her. He'd also told her she had a nice smile and that he enjoyed being with her because she never stressed about her size. Yep, she was a normal, healthy woman—kind to animals and small children. Most people liked her, yet the wretched man ignored her existence.

"Are you there, young lady?"

The querulous voice jerked Emma from her grievances re the lack of sex life back to her phone call. "I'm sorry. I had to sign for a courier parcel," she fibbed. "How can I help you?"

"My name is Elisa Denning. I need the services of a private investigator. Someone is stealing my prize rose blooms. Right before the flower show too. It's disgraceful. That's what it is."

"Let me take some details, then I'll arrange for an investigator to come and see you. Address? Telephone number?" Emma jotted down the woman's particulars, an imp inside her laughing as she imagined George assigning this case. None of the men would appreciate chasing a rose thief. George Taniwha's operatives preferred the dangerous stuff that challenged them and proved they were men.

Her humor died, replaced by a frown that drew her brows together. That was another thing she wanted to change. She'd passed all her private investigator exams. George had promised she'd be able to take on cases soon. Perhaps this one. Never let anyone say Emma Montrose didn't have ambition.

"When can I expect someone?" the elderly lady questioned. "I'm sure it's Mrs. Gibb's grandson, but the police won't do anything."

"An investigator will contact you tomorrow morning, Mrs. Denning."

"Excellent. Tomorrow is my baking day. I'll make them a cup of tea once they arrive."

Emma couldn't restrain a grin as a vision of one of George's tough he-man investigators drinking tea from a bone china cup popped into her mind. "I'm sure they'll enjoy refreshments. Thanks, Mrs. Denning." She disconnected and transcribed two proposals for prospective clients while she waited for Jack to leave George's office. She was smitten enough to want to gaze her fill as he departed since he had a truly fine butt.

The hands of the clock moved at the pace of a sick snail, and still Jack remained in George's inner sanctum. Reluctantly, Emma stood and packed up for the day. She grabbed her bag and couldn't prevent a glance at the closed door, searching for the tall, dark-haired man of her dreams.

Oh, yeah. No doubt about it. She was a sad, sad woman.

"I have a case for you," George said.

Something in his boss's tone, the watchful air in his sharp brown gaze made Jack cautious. "Yeah?"

"Sports-enhancing drugs. Rumor says there's a ring operating out of the Mahoney Resort on Waiheke Island in the Hauraki Gulf. I want you check it out."

"And?" Jack's gut told him there was more to the story. The twitch of George's lips confirmed his suspicions.

"I've assigned you a partner."

Jack straightened from his casual sprawl against the wall, his eyes narrowing on his middle-age boss. "I work alone. I don't work with a partner." His last one had died. Horribly. And he lived with that guilt. He wasn't damn well repeating the hellish experience.

"You can't do this job alone."

"Why not?" Jack demanded. "I've managed every other assignment on my own."

George leaned back in his chair, steepling his fingers and looking over the top in a thoughtful manner. While he appeared relaxed, Jack knew George would give him a tough battle should they ever decide to go the physical route during a disagreement. "This one might be a little difficult. Reuben J. Mahoney is a slippery character." The chair squeaked a protest each time the big man shifted his weight.

"I can handle anything he throws at me."

George glanced at the calendar pinned on the wall then cast his attention back to Jack. "There's a blue moon coming up. It might fall prior to the end of the case."

Jack filled in the blanks. The blue moon would erode his powers and make it difficult to retain his human form. Without constant sexual stimulation, he'd shift into a taniwha, the legendary dragon from Māori mythology. Jack snorted at the thought of being trapped in taniwha form in the middle of a mission. It had happened to other shifters on George Taniwha's staff but not to him. He imagined the pandemonium if he transformed in the middle of the bustling resort. A disdainful snort emerged.

Little did New Zealanders know, but the species taniwha survived and lived among them. Jack didn't intend to be the first taniwha to make headlines in the *New Zealand Herald*. No way. No how. If he had to find a woman to keep the monster at bay, then that was what he'd do.

"Okay," he conceded. "I guess a partner might help. Who's available? Hone? Billy?"

George issued a choking sound, merriment dancing across his lined face as he stuck his big-booted feet on his desk.

"What's so goddamn amusing?" Jack ground out.

Another chortle exploded from George.

Jack paced the length of the room, trying to combat the thrum of agitation working through his system. He paused to stare out the window, his mind taking in the yachts that zigzagged across blue waters of Auckland Harbor. Finally, he turned away and stalked back to drop into the chair opposite George. He kept his expression neutral despite the amusement still simmering across his boss's face. "You'd better let me in on the joke."

"You can partner up with Hone or Billy, if you want, but you might want to consider the special circumstances."

"What circumstances?" Hell, he had a hot date with Melissa tonight. Good, sweaty, no-strings sex. He didn't have time for this crap. "Either Hone or Billy. I'm not fussy."

"Reuben J. Mahoney runs a couples' resort. I'm assigning you a female partner."

"A female— *No*."

"I guess you can take Hone. Or Billy," George mused. "Of course, you'd have to share a room. And a bed." He shook his grizzled head. "Two taniwha in the same space. Add in a blue moon and things might get a mite ugly."

Fuck. Jack sent a hard glare at his boss. Trapped as neat as an eel in a net. Jack shuffled through the range of possibilities and came up blank. "Who is she?"

"A new operative."

Great. *Just bloody great*. Not only was he forced to take a female partner, he was getting a raw beginner. Jack didn't trust himself to speak so he firmed his mouth, folded his arms across his chest and scowled his displeasure.

"I'm teaming you with Emma Montrose."

"Your secretary?" Jack heard disbelief in his voice but thought he managed to keep his panic to himself. What the hell did a secretary know about investigating a case? What about the danger? To both of them. They would have to share a room, for God's sake. Jack refused to let his mind dwell on Emma's sexy legs...or the rest of her curvy form.

"Emma's capable of assisting you on this case."

"Assign me another case." Spending time alone with Emma was enough to give any hot-blooded male ideas. Jack wasn't interested in anything but sex. No relationships for him. Been there. Done that. Chucked away the T-shirt.

Nope. It was best he kept well away from the very curvy, brown-haired Emma Montrose. Every time he came into the office, her big blue eyes trailed after him like a pet dog expecting a treat, except instinct told him she had more in mind than stroking or petting. That was part of what caused his edginess whenever he was in her presence. A woman of Emma's caliber craved happily-ever-after.

Not his goal. Not anymore.

Some of the taniwha shifters—George, for example—were happily married, but finding a woman comfortable with her man turning into a dragon wasn't easy. It was a rare female who coped with the idea that her children might carry the taniwha gene. Or might not, depending on fate. The peculiarities of the taniwha species had rattled his ex-lover. She hadn't been able to cope with his *ugly appearance* and had run despite his assurances she would always remain human. He hadn't even reached the part about taniwha living longer—around thirty years longer—than the average human before his lover had run. Too late to tell her the benefit would extend to her.

"Did you say share a room?" Jack ignored the interested twitch from his cock.

"And a bed. But if you don't think you can act as part of a couple with Emma, I'll send Hone. He's due off assignment tomorrow."

Jack considered that for all of two seconds. He'd seen the way Hone looked at Emma. "I'll do it," he said, even though deep in his gut, he knew he'd regret this decision. "Give me the details."

The next morning, Emma marched into the offices of George Taniwha Investigators and Security, a woman on a mission. After spending her twenty-fifth birthday with her girlfriends and not one suitable male candidate in sight, she'd made a resolution. With the help of her tipsy friends, she'd decided to go for broke.

Get Jack Sullivan to notice her or bust.

A smile—was that too much to ask? No, dammit, it wasn't, and that would be just the start. She intended to progress from there—from a smile and good morning to down-and-dirty sex. Her breasts tingled at the thought and a swooping sensation spiraled to her lower belly. Of course, she wouldn't go as far as stalking, but she wasn't going to act the shy little wallflower either.

Emma Montrose was coming out of the shade and going after the man she wanted. She intended to channel the fictional taniwha on George Taniwha Investigators and Security's letterhead—formidable and determined, ready to scare Jack into thinking her way. By the time she was finished, he'd know of her interest. Then, he could take the next step.

She drew herself up.

No. That wasn't right.

She refused to let him slide from her sights without a fight. She'd take the second and third steps and as many other steps as the situation required.

Emma pushed aside several possible scenarios, concentrating on and visualizing the one she wanted. A secret smile curled across her lips as she fluffed her short curly hair.

Two lovers.

Emma and Jack.

Horizontal dancing.

Heat seeped into her cheeks. Emma yanked out her office wheelie chair, plonked down her butt and grabbed up a pile of envelopes off the desk to fan her face. This brave new Emma might embarrass her a little, but she'd try to keep up.

The front door of the office opened, and she straightened abruptly, her spine hitting the back of the chair. *Well.* No time like the present to put her plan into action.

Emma put her best receptionist manner into practice and flashed a smile. "Good morning, Jack."

The man froze in a possum-in-headlights pose, giving Emma the opportunity to look her fill. He was tall and built with a rower's powerful shoulders, slim hips and a butt that her fingers itched to grope. His hair was shiny black, halfway between short and long and in need of a cut, enticing her to smooth the messy strands away from his face. A dreamy sigh squeezed past her lips. Blessed with sun-kissed skin, no matter what the season, she often fantasized about his appearance beneath the layers of clothing. Did the gorgeous olive tones—a legacy from his Māori ancestors—extend all over his body? Hopefully she'd sit in a position of knowledge soon.

"Morning."

The word came out as a grunt, but it was an improvement on his usual silence or what she called the office furniture treatment. She forced away a surge of nerves and looked him straight in the eye. "Are you here to see George?"

"Yeah."

"Okay." Emma's breath caught, her lungs filling with his seductive scent—something that reminded her of the mystical Orient with hints of orange and patchouli and a healthy dose of masculine musk. She stared, and the act of holding his gaze propelled heat across her skin. A hot fiery surge of self-conscious emotion.

Dangerous.

Crazy.

A challenge to her goal.

She sucked in a deep breath and puffed it back out again. The sight of his gorgeous masculine attributes made a woman imagine skin-to-skin contact. That big, strong form moving against hers, thrusting deep into her pussy, callused hands fondling her breasts, fingers plucking at her nipples. A sensuous shiver swept her and arousal soaked her panties without warning.

She gulped and licked suddenly dry lips. All that from merely passing pleasantries. What would happen if they were naked? Together?

Get a grip, she thought sternly as her hormones danced a frenzied jitterbug. A cough cleared her throat. "I'll let him know you're here."

Hmmm. Not bad for the first time. She'd improve with the next meeting.

"I don't mind waiting."

Emma felt her eyes grow round. Huh? What was wrong with this picture?

Jack closed the distance between them and used his forefinger to tap her under the chin. Her heart stuttered in a mad gallop. She gasped, jerking from his touch in outright shock.

The door from the street burst open, and George bounded inside followed by his son, Hone. "Ah, you're here, Jack. I thought you might change your mind."

"No," Jack snapped, glaring at Hone.

Hone ignored Jack's scowl and sauntered across the office to stop beside Emma. "Hello, sweetheart." He hauled her from her chair and wrapped her in a breath-stealing bear hug.

"Put her down," Jack growled.

"But I haven't seen her for a week." Hone nuzzled her neck and Emma giggled. "She's my girl."

"Don't you have a case to solve?" Jack looked as if he wanted to punch his friend.

Not in the least perturbed by his buddy's bad temper, Hone parked his butt on the corner of her desk and flashed a sexy grin. Emma sighed as she peeked through lowered lashes at Jack's surly face. Why couldn't she fall for Hone instead of grumpy Jack? It was a mystery, all right. Although Hone made her smile and was easy on the eye, he didn't affect her heart rate in the slightest.

Not like Jack.

George shook his head. "Hone, I want you to check into a case that came in yesterday. Mrs. Denning has a thief she needs to flush out. Emma can give you the details. Jack, I want to go over a few details regarding the case we discussed yesterday." He strode toward his office but paused in the doorway. "Emma, I need to see you in my office once you're finished with Hone."

Bother. She'd hoped George might let her gain some practical experience with Mrs. Denning's case. Obviously not. She scowled and decided it was time to remind George of his promise.

Five minutes later, Emma knocked lightly on George's door and entered. She carried a pad and pen to take notes. Jack was sprawled in a chair near the window. He jumped to his feet on seeing her.

"Ah, good." George checked his watch then stood. "I have a golf date. I'll leave you in Jack's capable hands."

George's words echoed in her mind for long drawn-out seconds. She heard the click of the door as her boss departed but couldn't concentrate on anything except the concept of capable hands. A mental picture popped into her mind, aided by fertile imagination. Masculine hands cupping her naked breasts, fingers plucking her sensitive nipples.

Oh, my. She subsided into a chair in case her legs buckled. Without warning, her cotton blouse felt several sizes too small and her face glowed with enough heat to cook a batch of pikelets for morning tea. She fanned her cheeks vigorously with her notepad.

"Are you feeling all right?" Emma's head snapped up to find Jack's enigmatic gaze settled on her. "You'll be as useful as a war canoe without a warrior to paddle if you fall sick."

"What...what do you mean?" Emma thought she understood but wanted clarity and confirmation.

"George wants you to help me with my case."

Emma jumped to her feet and pumped her fist in the air. "Yes!" She did an impromptu jig before noticing his gaze on her bouncing breasts. Emma froze then dropped into her chair, striving to keep embarrassment from crawling across her face. She *must* work on maintaining her cool.

"Don't get too excited. You're along on a trial basis. You help out with the grunt work. Do what I say, when I say with no questions asked. Is that clear?"

"No problem." Emma restrained her celebratory grin and the urge to give him a cheeky salute. *Hot damn.* She was gonna be a private dick. "What's the case?"

"We're investigating at the Mahoney Resort over on Waiheke Island. We think there's a drug ring running out of the resort. Sports-enhancing drugs."

"Sounds great. Are we going for the day? When are we going?" Emma was finding it difficult to sit still instead of dancing in celebration. Her first case and closer contact with Jack all in one hit. Life couldn't get much better.

Jack scowled, a fierce frown, no doubt in an attempt to burst her bubble of enthusiasm. "We're going for a week. You'll need to pack tonight since we leave for Waiheke tomorrow. Here's the file. Read the documents carefully and let me know if you have questions."

Emma nodded eagerly. Their hands brushed during the file transfer and a frisson of pleasure zapped down her arm. Surprised, she jerked away, almost dropping the info in her haste. "I'll read it," she promised, her gaze lowering to screen her reaction. Her stomach swooped and plunged as if she were attached to a bungee cord. Aware of the burgeoning silence and Jack's disapproval, she hurried into speech. "What time do we leave?"

"The ferry departs at ten tomorrow morning. I'll pick you up at nine thirty."

"I live at—"

"I know your address. Don't be late."

CHAPTER 2

Anticipation heated her cheeks and zipped to her belly as they joined the queue to board the ferry to Mahoney's island resort. She swallowed, hoping to settle the swarm of butterflies inhabiting her stomach. It was happening. She was actually taking part in an investigation.

Emma shuffled from foot to foot, picking up her bag then setting it back down while she tried to take in everything and quell her impatience to get started. She glanced at Jack. Calm. Uninterested even. He acted so unaffected while everyone else radiated excitement. Very strange.

Animated chatter filled the covered walkway where they waited to board. A hostess dressed in black shorts and a tight pale blue T-shirt emblazoned with the word *Mahoney's* in navy blue over her left breast, checked people off her list and allowed them to board. Couples of all ages and sizes lined up, shuffling hand luggage and making friends with strangers in the line.

No one talked to them.

Not that Emma blamed anyone. Jack could appear scary to the uninitiated with his unruly dark hair and the dragon tattoo that wound around his left biceps.

Of course, there were some who saw past the tough-guy disguise. Emma knew he gave up his time to help out at a local foster home. She knew there was gentleness beneath the grumpy exterior, but he kept it well hidden.

Deep in thought, she leaped in fright when a masculine arm curved around her waist.

"You're gonna have to cure the jumpiness. We're meant to be lovers."

Emma's gaze shot up to meet dark chocolate-brown eyes. *Sinful eyes*, she thought with an inward sigh.

Those eyes could lead her into transgressions. *Anytime.*

"Sure, honey," Emma said, miffed for almost giving them away. Yet she was angry with Jack, too, because he was doing his best to shove her off balance. He'd certainly tried to talk her out of the assignment. She wanted to glare but it wasn't loverlike. Most of all she wanted to needle Jack into some sort of response. Anything. Yes, an urge to poke him with a sharp stick just to witness his reaction had her fingers flexing.

"How long before we get to our room?" she cooed instead, fluttering her mascara-laden lashes at him. "I need your cock inside me." Part of Emma was shocked at her words, but the couple standing in front of them grinned at her in sympathy.

"Have you seen the contents of those goody bags the hostess is giving out?" the young blonde woman asked. A theatrical shiver jiggled her pert, braless breasts.

"No, what?" Emma's fertile imagination created all sorts of pictures. Handcuffs? Powerful aphrodisiacs? Torturous sex toys?

The woman leaned closer to whisper, "A pair of edible undies."

"Both his and hers," her partner added with a grin.

"No!" Emma breathed. *Good grief.* It would be akin to choking down pills. With her luck, she'd gag and throw up all over her lover's groin. All over Jack's groin. "I hope they're chocolate flavored." Emma waggled her brows.

"Oh, you're terrible." The woman giggled.

So terrible that Jack's arm tightened around her in silent warning, his fingers digging into the sensitive flesh at her waist. She smothered a grin. Perhaps if she kept needling him, her nervousness would pass.

"I'm looking forward to this week," she confided to the young woman. "My honey works so hard. He's exhausted when he gets home, and most nights, he falls asleep in his chair watching television." She slid a glance his way to gauge Jack's reaction. Her stomach flipped anxiously on noticing the tic in his shadowed jaw.

He looked as though he might burst while the arm around her waist tensed until it resembled a shackle. But not enough to make her stop goading him. "Too tired for good sex, if you know what I mean."

A low growl vibrated through his chest. Emma stilled and the back of her neck prickled. Slowly, her gaze rose from his broad chest and traveled up his neck, across his rigid jaw to collide with stormy eyes.

"We intend to make up for that, don't we, sweetheart?" His pinched expression promised retribution. "Can't have you saying I don't keep you satisfied. Wouldn't want you to wander to other men."

Oops. Perhaps she'd pushed a little hard.

The line moved, and Emma nudged her bag forward with her foot. She was very conscious of Jack standing close behind her.

The hostess beamed at them. "Hello and welcome. Names, please."

"Jack Sullivan and Emma Montrose." Jack stepped abreast of her, taking control and smiling at the hostess.

"Ah, yes. Here we go. Here are your goody bags." The hostess handed a violet canvas bag to each of them. "Your room assignment and everything you need to know about the resort is in there along with a few surprises."

"Thanks." Emma grasped the purple cord handle, a tremor apparent as she stepped over an invisible line—a gateway into sin.

She glanced at Jack to find him eyeing her with an inscrutable expression. Emma's mouth firmed with determination, and her chin shot upward. She could do this. She *would* do this despite Jack's silent censure. She intended to complete this assignment to the best of her ability. And, if she managed to make Jack notice her as a female, a hot sexual being, so much the better.

The woman was driving him to drink. In her brief red shorts, and her figure-hugging white shirt, she was a menace to clear thinking. Jack glared at her back as she sashayed along the gangplank to board the ferry. His gaze drifted to her curvy butt, encased in the tight shorts. With the enhanced hearing all taniwhas possessed, he heard the rapid beat of her heart. She wanted him. Suddenly, he had a hard-on to beat all. Deep inside his mind, the dragon clawed for release.

Sweat beaded on his forehead. His head started to swim in an alarming manner. Hell, he couldn't shift here. Not now, in front of these people. The demand of the dragon pounded him until he trembled with the desire to change to taniwha form or to fuck a woman. Any woman. In the dragon's mind, these were the sole alternatives.

Jack knew better.

Desperation made his fists bunch and his chest heave as he tried to force oxygen into starved lungs. Concentrate. Focus on something else. *Block.*

In his mind, he pictured his cat—the scrawny stray that should have known better than to seek refuge with a dragon who wasn't a vegetarian. The cat had kept coming around anyway. Though damn if he knew when the arrogant black tom had become his cat. Jack snorted under his breath, cursing the taniwha that struggled for dominance. He focused, forcing his mind to change track.

The cat had probably won him over about the time he'd presented Jack with a huge eel in the middle of the night. A gift of the highest magnitude. Yes, that had been the defining moment. Jack centered his mind on the scruffy black cat and fought the dragon that writhed under his skin. The dragon roared in displeasure, the sound echoing through his head. He ached to feel the cool waters of the harbor, the explosive release of sex equally compelling.

You can't damn well have sex, Jack shouted silently. *Behave, dammit.* Shit, no wonder he had a headache.

"Are you all right?" A slender hand with pale pink nails touched his forearm. Jack started, his nostrils flaring as her clean floral scent washed over him. His dragon fought briefly then retreated with a snarl.

"Thinking about the case." Jack didn't relax an iota. How could he when Emma's wide-eyed expression screamed innocence? The scent of lavender and roses backed up the veneer of inexperience along with the baby-pink polish painted on her finger and toenails. His gaze drifted up to meet hers.

Whoa, baby. No way was her avid gaze innocent. She puckered her pink lips then her tongue slid out to moisten the plump curves. The dragon roared approval, and his cock stirred again with definite interest. *Well, hell*.

Emma's intriguing mix of artlessness and pure sex appeal knocked away his ability to remain detached. This assignment might be the death of him. The dragon wouldn't let him forget her willingness. Perhaps he should've brought the damn cat with him because he was going to be focusing on the furry creature a lot—just in self-defense.

Jack guided Emma to the bow of the boat. It was crowded at present, but once they pulled from the sheltered harbor into the Gulf, the cool sea air and brisk wind would send the passengers scurrying for the warmth of the lounge and bar area. He edged her to the railing and caged her in place with his arms.

Emma jumped and barely bit back a nervous schoolgirl *eep*. Jack, of course, registered her reaction.

"Quit that. Remember you're playing the part of my partner."

"I hate that word." Emma glanced over her shoulder at him. "What does that mean? When someone refers to their partner."

He crowded her, gritting his teeth as his cock brushed her ass. "Would you prefer lover?" He relished her shiver, and satisfaction filled him as she tried to edge away. "Take care. We don't want people to think we're arguing."

The number of passengers boarding slowed to a trickle then

stopped. Finally, the deckhands released the moorings and the ferry slipped from the berth. Excited chatter filled the deck area where they stood. Jack scanned faces and bodies. Despite the breeze, most of the women were dressed in a similar manner to Emma—shorts and skimpy T-shirts or thin cotton shirts. Shouldn't be long before they beat a retreat inside out of the wind.

"I thought the weather forecast said fine and sunny." Emma tried to move. "Can we go inside? It's cold."

"I want to discuss the case. Work out a plan of attack." Jack pulled her against his chest and wrapped his arms around her. The taniwha stirred, sighing in pleasure. Jack ruthlessly erected a barrier in his mind, forcing the beast back. Then Jack exhaled too, pushing away the hum of pleasure as her scent filled his senses. No doubt about it. Emma fit his arms perfectly.

"Okay, so talk."

"This is a job, and that's all. Don't get any romantic ideas just because we're posing as a couple. I'm not interested in anything but getting the job done." Emma froze in his arms, and he wished he could see her expression. Instead, she stared directly ahead at the dormant volcanic island of Rangitoto.

"Of course, I understand." Her voice emerged clear but stiff.

"Good." Jack should've experienced relief, but instead he felt as if he'd kicked a puppy. However, he'd achieved his goal. She wouldn't harbor a single romantic illusion about them becoming a real couple.

An hour later, the hostess led them from the resort reception area. She pushed the door open and stood back to let them enter their accommodation.

"There's only one bed," Emma blurted.

The hostess gaped at her in bemusement, making Emma realize her error. Of course, they'd be expected to share a bed. This was a week for couples and sex. After all, her mind dwelt on sex.

"He snores dreadfully," she told the hostess, taking petty revenge for the hurt he'd inflicted on her earlier. *Just a job. No romantic ideas*, she mocked silently as she detoured around the bags the porter deposited in the middle of the floor. No romantic ideas for her. All she wanted was sex—the hot and sweaty kind. "I suppose I can always pull out the earplugs as a last resort."

"I do not—"

Emma stepped closer to Jack and gave in to the temptation to run her fingers through his hair. The dark locks slithered against her skin—soft and silky and smelling of the sea. Wow, even better than her imagination. "Of course you do, but that's part of your charm. Too many good points and I'd get bored. I mean you're excellent at sex. Superior. Great stamina. What more could I ask of a lover?"

Jack made a choking sound deep in his throat as she trailed a hand across his broad chest. Her fingers tingled while her pulse leapt at her daring.

"Can I help with anything else?" the hostess asked, amusement coloring her voice. "Remember, the welcome party starts promptly at midday. It's just a short meeting so we can outline the activities for the week. After that, you're free for the rest of the day to partake in all the facilities we have at the resort. We want you to be rested for our gala dinner tonight."

"Thanks." Emma continued with her exploration while she had Jack captive and within touching distance. "We have everything we need."

The door swung shut with a soft click.

"That's enough," Jack growled. "She's gone now."

Emma drew a sharp breath, gathering her courage. "You need to kiss me."

"What?"

Was that panic in his dark eyes? "We're meant to be a couple," she explained, starting to enjoy herself. "We'll have to kiss at some stage to make sure we look the part. I think we should practice. We don't want to give ourselves away." Her heart thundered and blood heated every inch of skin. She was hyperaware of his strength and masculinity.

Jack glanced at her and immediately her lips tingled. His chest rose as he sucked in an audible breath. Yep, she'd definitely put the fear of God into him. His mouth worked, but no words emerged, then he grabbed her. Their lips smashed together and parted just as quickly. Jack jerked away, and they stared at each other, both breathing hard.

"That was not a kiss." Emma broke the pregnant silence. Frustration washed through her, leaving her feeling cheated. Her mission was turning out trickier than she'd envisaged.

Jack scowled. She presumed he meant to frighten her in the same way he scared everyone else he encountered. It wouldn't work. She was on to him. "Come here. I want to show you how we should kiss in public."

When he remained motionless, she closed the distance between them. She placed her hands on his shoulders. The muscles and tendons were tense and chilly apart from his dragon tattoo. For some reason the black ink design radiated heat. "You're very cold."

"Get it over with." Jack's hard smile held enough temper to warn her not to push him any longer.

She stood on tiptoe and gingerly claimed a kiss. He didn't budge but didn't cooperate either. Time to move this experiment along. Emma opened her mouth and made contact with her tongue. A groan rumbled deep in his chest. *Oh, yeah!* Score one for the home team. Working on pure instinct, she moved her lips persuasively against his. She nibbled, then soothed the tiny nips with a sensual lick.

Jack's arms circled her without warning, and he tugged her

off-balance until his muscular chest flattened her breasts. He tipped her head back and moved his mouth over hers with toe-curling expertise. She gasped, taking in his masculine flavor, a hint of mint and the tang of the sea. He tasted good, so good. Then his tongue slipped inside to twine with hers, and she became officially addicted. Her breasts peaked against her bra as their mouths slid together in a sensuous dance.

Jack pressed closer and to her delight, she discovered he was interested. *A hard-on.* With a subtle twitch of her hips, she shifted against his sizeable erection. Her eyes fluttered shut to savor both the sensation and her triumph. Emma Montrose had turned on big, bad Jack Sullivan.

Jack pulled away as abruptly as he'd grabbed her. They stared at each other for a long drawn-out moment. She moistened her lips and his dark gaze followed the movement. *Game, set and match, bad boy.*

"Right." He straightened and took a giant step away from her. "We've established we can manage a kiss without looking as if we've never done it before." He glared at her, obviously in an attempt to regain control. She wasn't about to relinquish her advantage, no matter how much he glowered.

His body was interested in sex.

Sex with her.

All she needed to do was push harder until he crumpled.

Without warning, doubt flitted through her mind, sinking

tendrils deep. Could she act with sexual aggression? She quashed the negative thought. Nah, men were easy. And damn if she would turn twenty-six without knowing sexual pleasure with Jack.

Jack glanced at the diver's watch on his wrist. "We'd better go to this blasted meeting. While we're there, I want you to take note of the faces. If there's anyone you think is familiar or is mentioned in the file, take note and tell me later."

Emma nodded. "I'll just change before we go. I thought I'd check out the pool after the meeting."

Jack observed the sway of her hips as she walked over to her bag and rummaged through the contents. She fished out something small enough to hide in her fisted hand, then sashayed into the en suite and closed the door. His dragon released a low growl of need.

"Fuck." He rubbed the heels of his hands over his eyes and dragged in a huge breath. He was in trouble and was man—taniwha—enough to admit it. What the hell had happened to the brown sparrow from the office?

The creak of the door jerked him upright. He turned and experienced an instant roar of approval from the taniwha. This was no brown sparrow standing proudly in front of him. Emma Montrose was one curvy, confident, sexy woman and she scared the crap out of him. Her breasts were poured into an itty-bitty red top that barely contained them. Then there were acres of smooth, pale skin before his gaze hit the brief bikini panties shielding her femininity. With her Marilyn Monroe figure, she reminded him of the curvy film stars of the fifties. Add in a little more height and you got Emma Montrose—a luscious armful of femininity.

"Is that all you're wearing?"

"I have a sarong." She grabbed a square of red-and-white patterned material from her bag, wrapped it around her hips and tied it with a knot. "I think I'll buy another from the gift store to take home as a souvenir."

"What about a thing for the top? A towel?" He gestured at her breasts in their itty-bitty top. Anything to screen her lush curves from his sight.

Emma tossed her head. "I'll get a towel at the pool."

"Won't you get cold?"

This time, Emma shrugged and her breasts jiggled enough to distract him. "The sun has come out and it looks as though the wind has died. Besides, the brochure says there's nude bathing—"

Jack ripped his gaze from her cleavage to stare at her in shock. "Over my dead body."

Emma planned to be difficult. The defiant tilt of her chin confirmed her obstinate gene. How had he missed her stubbornness? She'd always scuttled out of his way, giving a creditable impression of a frightened bird.

This Emma was no sparrow.

Jack jerked open the door and stood back. "Let's go."

She exited with a sashay, the pert wiggle of her hips drawing his eye. Sweat coated his skin while his cock jumped to high alert. Jack debated his reaction. Curse a blue streak or laugh hysterically? One thing was for sure. They couldn't share a room without the simmering attraction between them boiling over. *Oh, yeah*. No wonder George had belly laughed. His boss had probably noticed Emma's crush. The joke was well and truly on him.

Jack followed her along the brightly lit corridor and outside.

The sea, pungent and briny, called its siren song, trying to entice him to shift and slip into the cool waters. He forced himself to concentrate. Instead of facing temptation tonight, he'd wait for Emma to fall asleep, then leave to do some investigating. With luck, he'd be able to check out Mahoney's office and find something to further their investigation. Or blow the whole case wide open so he could save his taniwha butt and hightail it home to his scruffy tomcat and safety.

Emma paused by a garden full of colorful blooms. She trailed a hand over the lavender border. "Do you prefer to swim in a pool or the sea?"

"The sea."

"You live by the sea, don't you?"

"Yeah."

She made a small huffing sound. "Do you live by yourself?"

"Yeah."

"No pets?"

"I have a cat. What's with the questions?"

"I'm your significant other. I should know these things. I live by myself but have loads of friends. I hate swimming in the sea—long story, but I almost drowned. I'll tell you one day. I'm twenty-five years old and my favorite food is hokey pokey ice cream. Oh, and chocolate. I love chocolate."

"This is where the meeting's taking place." Jack opened the door and ushered her inside, relieved to end the questions. There was one thing worth knowing about a woman and that was how easy she was to bed. As a taniwha, he needed that type of information. He did *not* need to know her personal likes and dislikes.

The large meeting space was packed to capacity and most of the women were dressed in similar outfits to Emma's. In fact, Jack felt distinctly overdressed in his shirt and shorts.

Jack directed her toward two empty chairs and settled at Emma's side. He scanned the men and women sitting either side. Damn, crowds made him antsy. They were so bloody happy. Shit, make that horny. He could hear their rapid heartbeats and their naughty whispering. The majority of them looked as if they needed a bedroom.

He glanced at Emma, and saw the sexy flush on her cheeks, the kiss-swollen lips. Fuck, he didn't need this distraction. Jack forced his mind back to the job. Given the opportunity tonight, he'd scour the island, check out the private marina and wharf.

A young woman walked up to a microphone, followed by several others. All of them, except one—an older man—were dressed in a uniform of black shorts and blue T-shirts.

"Good afternoon!" the man shouted.

Well, damn. Jack sat up straighter on recognizing him once he turned in their direction. Rueben J. Mahoney himself. *Interesting.* The owner wasn't always at the resort. His presence made the back of Jack's neck prickle in the way it did when an investigation was advancing.

"Welcome to Mahoney Resort. We have a great week planned with lots of naughty fun especially for couples!" A roar of approval greeted Mahoney's words. "I know you're anxious to begin your holiday, so I'll hand you over to Lissa."

"Welcome! Sounds as if you're ready to party." With a laugh, Lissa—a bubbly redhead—held up her right hand in a bid for silence. "To start the fun, I want you to look under your chairs. Two lucky people should find a red heart sticker."

A buzz of chatter rippled free as everyone stood to peer under their chairs.

"I've got one!" Emma shrieked.

Jack winced. "That figures."

"Could the two lucky winners come up here to collect their prizes? We have a bag full of sex toys and games for you to spice up your week."

Emma bounded up to the stage with the red sticker clutched in her hand. A man in his fifties followed hot on her heels.

Jack swallowed a groan when one of hostesses on the stage

presented Emma with her prize. Reuben J. Mahoney kissed her on the cheek and tossed her a joking remark. Jack gritted his teeth as he heard the drawl of the man's voice but not the actual words.

The desire to curse and shock the hell out of the little old lady and her bright-eyed husband sitting next to them rode Jack like a demon jockey with spurs. Contrarily, the dragon roared with excitement and anticipation. Bit by bit, his strength and determination to stay the heck out of Emma's panties was being eroded. Jack sighed and finally accepted the truth.

He was a dead man, but at least he was gonna die happy.

CHAPTER 3

E mma blinked at him in an innocent manner. "It wasn't my fault I won the spot prize."

Jack suspected she wasn't the slightest bit sorry. The twinkle in her blue eyes spoke of mischievous pleasure, and her attitude rubbed against his horny taniwha.

"What are we going to do now?"

"I am going to do a reconnaissance of the resort. I thought you were going to the pool."

Her bright smile dimmed before bursting into life again. The sight flipped his stomach with foreboding. What the hell was she up to now?

"I think I'll go to the beach instead of the pool." She lifted the large package and waved it in front of him. "Not to swim. I can sunbathe and check out my loot."

Jack froze and slowly nodded. She couldn't come to much harm on the beach.

One hour later, Jack finished his quick whistle-stop tour of the resort. He checked out the gym, the swimming pool with the spa pools and sauna facilities. There was a health spa he'd poked his head inside, then promptly retreated but not fast enough. As an excuse he'd ended up making an appointment for Emma for a massage and something to do with seaweed before he could escape.

He'd checked out the golf course, the archery area, and the petanque pit, where guests played the French version of outdoor bowls. Then, he'd hit one of the walking tracks that skirted the property and led to Stoney Batter—the World War II gun placements and connecting tunnels—if a guest was willing to trek for two hours. He discovered several other paths of various lengths, which led to points of interest, along with tennis courts and numerous water sports available to entertain the guests.

The private beach stretched the length of the resort golf course. At the end of the beach, a river mouth emptied into the sea, the sand changing to thick river mud. Hundreds of mangrove trees grew in the oozing sludge. They were full of bird life but not very hospitable for humans.

The resort covered a lot of ground—a fact that made Jack's life difficult because it would be easy for a drug ring to operate without detection. He made a mental note to check for day guests.

Jack turned toward the beach to search for Emma. The sand crunched under his sandals once he stepped off the footpath. The surge and retreat of the waves lulled him as he scanned the vicinity. Halfway along the beach, four males crowded around a beach towel. He caught a low drone as one of them spoke and the answering feminine laugh.

Emma.

Jealousy struck hard and without warning. His steps lengthened, and his taniwha growled in displeasure, ready to kick butt.

"Emma, there you are." He kept his voice low and even—or tried to. His dragon let loose with a roar that squeezed past his control before he could blink.

The four men visibly backed away from Emma.

She sent him a chiding look and pursed her rosebud pink lips. "Darling, this is Carlos, Daniel, Justin and Doug. They wanted to know what I'd won in my prize."

Jack made a concerted effort to contain his displeasure, but unsuccessfully since the four men retreated farther from their previous huddle around Emma.

"We'd better get back to the bar. The girls should have finished in the spa by now," one of them said after they'd exchanged wary glances.

"Nice to meet you." Emma beamed. "And thanks for the hints. I'm sure they'll come in handy."

"See you 'round," another of the men said.

Jack managed a brief nod of acknowledgment and waited in broody silence until they left. He yanked his shirt over his head and dropped onto the sand beside her. All it took was one look and he almost drooled. She smelled of coconut lotion and her skin gleamed, drawing his gaze to the red top and her plump breasts.

"You could have been a bit more polite."

"Why? What hints?" If she wanted sex tips, she should ask him.

"About the best way to use some of the toys I won. Do you have some input for me?"

Jack went from pissed to boiling hot in seconds flat. The woman had a smart mouth and he was just the man to cure her of the malady. He sprang, pushing her down until she lay full length on her towel. A small *oomph* escaped her as he covered her, squashing her breasts against his bare chest. He thrust his thigh between her legs to hold her in place, ignoring the squeak of surprise.

She opened her mouth, probably to complain, but he halted any protests by plundering her lips, sliding his tongue into the moist cavern beyond, just as his taniwha demanded.

She froze, then softened beneath him, her hands gripping his shoulders to hold him closer. Her fingers slid across his back then lower to cup his arse.

Jack ripped his mouth away from hers. "What the devil are you doing?"

"I've wanted to cop a feel of your butt for ages," she confessed a trifle breathlessly. "It's...ah...very nice."

The sensation of her hands sliding over him, even though he wore shorts, sent his libido soaring into overdrive. His cock hardened with painful intensity until it felt as though his shorts were several sizes too small. A groan formed deep in his chest and without conscious thought, he started a little exploration of his own.

Smooth skin greeted his touch. He trailed his fingertips across her rib cage and higher to cup one breast. The hands on his butt stilled and when their gazes connected, he saw her wide eyes held a trace of shock. Jack traced the edge of her itty-bitty top with a forefinger then dipped beneath the tight fabric to the smooth flesh beneath. Maintaining her gaze, he leaned over and let his tongue trace the same path. Her scent filled his nostrils—the same lavender and roses he'd noticed earlier plus coconut from her suntan lotion—as he licked over the slope of one breast.

Not enough. Not nearly enough. He peeled the red material from her breasts, revealing taut pink nipples to the afternoon sun and his gaze. Proud and full breasts that enticed and enthralled him.

She made a tiny sound. Jack couldn't decide whether it was shock or one of encouragement.

Then her lips parted and white teeth flashed in a grin full of challenge. "You gonna stop there?" She rolled slightly, reached behind her back, and Jack heard the faint click of her bikini top closure. The red fabric slid down her arms. A shrug made the material fall away, leaving her topless and vulnerable to his gaze.

A breath hissed through his teeth. He couldn't have stopped to save himself. His heart thundered, and his taniwha stretched and stirred, prodding him to continue. Slowly, he lowered his head to take one pink nipple in his mouth. Jack closed his lips around the taut peak, the need to do everything all at once riding him hard. Like a man who hadn't eaten for days, he feasted. Savoring the flavor of her—the texture. Gently biting. Tasting her and tormenting himself with her silky skin and sinful curves.

Dicing with danger.

Emma cradled his head, her fingers entwining in his hair, urging him onward. He drew hard on her nipple, and she bucked beneath him, brushing against his groin.

"Harder," she murmured in a dreamy voice. "That feels so good." Emma had no pretense in her. She was innocence and honesty wrapped in a bow.

And he wanted to take this to a conclusion. Jack pulled away far enough to scrutinize her face. Her eyes were closed, and her lips curled up in a dreamy smile. That smile jerked him back to reality.

Jack rolled away, trying to ignore the gleam of her nipples, still wet from his mouth. He wasn't interested in anything more than a roll in the sack. Getting his rocks off.

"We'd better go." He stood and handed his shirt to her so she could cover up. "We have a job to do. Mucking about on the beach isn't getting it done. Besides, we've got this dinner thing."

"I can't believe it," Jack muttered, glancing at the huge box Emma carried. He rolled his eyes while the taniwha inside stomped a Māori war dance and combined it with a few exuberant high kicks, judging by the feel of his bouncing gut. A year's supply of condoms. "I've never met anyone with such dumb luck."

"I can't help it," Emma said cheerfully without a trace of remorse or embarrassment.

Hell, no. He'd been the one who'd caught the flack. Lots of jokes and pats on the back—all with the same message. He should eat lots to keep up his strength. Sure, it was all in good fun, but the sly innuendo wore thin after a while.

Worst of all, Emma's win had called attention to them. Everyone in the whole damn resort would recognize their faces. It was difficult to skulk around on an investigation when everyone was busy snickering.

"What are you going to do with a year's supply of condoms anyway?"

"Use them," Emma said sweetly.

Jack's fists clenched at his sides, and he felt as if someone had kicked him in the gut. The thought of Emma using the condoms with another man fueled his temper—not that using them with him was a better proposition. This afternoon had been a mistake. He wasn't going to touch her again. She was commitment through and through. He was free and easy—a different species of fish altogether.

Jack opened the restaurant door for Emma and stood back as she sashayed into the night air in her short black dress, which showed far too much skin for his liking. Gritting his teeth, he stalked after her. Colored lights lit both sides of the path that wound between lush plantings of native ferns and trees and strategically placed rock carvings.

In the bush on the far side of the resort, a lone morepork cried. Its mournful call echoed through the still night. Jack heard the rustle of small creatures scurrying for cover from the owl. Waves rolled into the shore interspersed by laughing and shouting from the couples still celebrating in the bar after the gala dinner.

Even though it was almost one in the morning, he'd have to hang with Emma to give everyone time to settle in for the night. It was either that or hit the bar. He shot a glance at his partner. Temptation shot through him, fast and hard. He wanted her. Perhaps a drink would be the better option.

"Emma, wait up."

She paused and turned to look at him. That bloody box of condoms taunted him without mercy. "I'm going to the bar to check out who's there. I want to see if the staff will talk to me."

"Should I come?"

Yes, please. Preferably with me inside your tight pussy. "No!" he snapped, appalled at his wayward thoughts. Bloody hell, he couldn't blame his dragon. That was the last thing he needed—to smell her flowery scent and hear each hitch of her breath. He needed sex tonight. That was the only way he could exert control over the taniwha and continue to work with Emma. "I'll escort you to our room and head back to the bar."

"I could help."

"I thought you'd agreed to follow my orders?"

"Hmmm." She had the audacity to raise one shapely eyebrow and let the corners of her mouth drift upward in the beginnings of a smile.

Jack grabbed her by the elbow and hustled her on their way. Two minutes later, he pulled a keycard out of his pocket and slid it into the door. He slipped the keycard into the wall socket and a single light came on, spotlighting the bed. The rich burgundy cover gleamed, decadent and suggestive of sex.

Jack froze. If he were a superstitious man, he'd think someone was trying to tell him something.

Condoms.

Bed.

Emma.

The ingredients were present. All he needed to do was stop fighting and go with the flow.

Then he heard a scraping noise, soft and out of place. He

prowled into the center of the floor space, trying to isolate where the vibration had originated.

Emma sat on the corner of the bed and bent to slip off her strappy black shoes. The soft sigh she made when she wriggled her toes pulled his cock tight and tented his black trousers.

Surreptitiously, he searched the walls and contents for anything out of place or remotely suspicious. Feet shuffled and it sounded as if someone fidgeted. Jack cocked his head, listening for the slightest vibration but couldn't pinpoint the sound with accuracy. It came from near the in-room bar. Nothing seemed disturbed yet the back of his neck prickled. He snarled beneath his breath, allowing his taniwha senses free rein or as much as he could with a human nearby. Gradually, he filtered out the small sounds made by Emma as she removed her jacket and kicked her shoes out of the way. He sauntered over to the minibar.

"Want a drink?" Jack continued to scan the area, his gaze skimming a large mirror hanging on the wall near the bar. Standing this close, two dark shapes were discernible to his acute vision. They were behind the mirror. He tensed and forced himself to relax. A two-way mirror directly in line with the bed.

"No, drink for me, thanks. I thought you were going to the bar."

"Soon." The distinct crackle of wrapping paper momentarily shifted his attention. "What are you doing?" To his critical ear, his voice sounded harsh and a touch defensive.

Damn, he was losing control of this assignment and he loathed the feeling. Sex dominated his thoughts. He winged a glare at the mirror—a bloody two-way one to complicate their case. Aware his famed control was fraying, he took a deep breath and fixed himself a whiskey. He tipped back his head and let the alcohol slide down his throat. Although the peaty flavor tasted good, the burn didn't do a thing to soothe his irritation.

The two watchers remained, and Jack couldn't decide whether they'd lucked out and scored a room specially set up for voyeurs, or if their cover was blown and they were under surveillance for more sinister reasons.

He poured another finger of whiskey and stared into the amber depths in broody silence.

"There are six different types of condoms in here along with two types of lubricant." Emma sounded breathless as if she expected him to respond.

And dammit all—he wanted to react.

Perhaps that was the solution. They could reassure the voyeurs by having hot, sweaty sex. Just one bout, he told himself. He glanced at Emma and found her still exploring the contents of her package. She'd tried to do it before but he hadn't given her the opportunity. His mind grouped sex and Emma in the same sentence too often as it was without looking at visual props.

"Ohhh." Her small breathy sigh snared his attention, mainly because it reminded him of sex. But then, everything reminded him of the act when it involved Emma.

"Do people really use these?" she asked, extending something in her palm for him to see.

Two pastel-colored hearts lay in her palm. Each bore a suggestion.

Lick my pussy.

Suck my cock.

His taniwha roared at him to grab her, to hammer into her body until they were both satisfied. Jack forced himself to glance away and study the dregs of whiskey in his glass.

Sex with Emma. He flirted with the idea and the possible repercussions. His dragon clawed for sexual appeasement, and Jack knew he'd have to give in or shift and scare the living daylights out of Emma and their silent watchers.

George Taniwha Investigators and Security couldn't afford the publicity—that was a given. The hand holding his glass started to itch insistently. When he glanced down, Jack saw the sheen of forming scales. That settled his dilemma.

They'd have sex.

He was a professional. He could do this—remain detached and get the job done. Sex was only an exchange of bodily fluids.

Decision made, he swallowed the last mouthful of whiskey and placed the glass on the bar top with a decisive click. His hands went to the buttons on his shirt. He unfastened them rapidly, shrugged from the blue cotton shirt and tossed it aside. He stepped out of his black trousers and chucked them in the direction of his shirt.

"What are you doing?"

Not a shred of fear showed in her expression. A good thing, although he never employed force. He'd show her the goods and gauge her reaction. Then, he'd give her one last chance to say no.

Jack slid his fingers under the elastic band of his black boxer-briefs. A growl of excitement escaped the taniwha.

Emma's eyes widened at the low, rumbling growl. He pushed the boxers over his fully erect shaft. Her mouth dropped open as she continued to stare. At least she hadn't screamed and run from the room.

Jack sauntered closer to the bed. "What does it look like I'm doing?"

The ambiance throbbed with silence. Even the two watchers had stopped their fidgeting to concentrate on the action in the bedroom. Jack hoped they were enjoying the view of his bare arse.

Emma licked her lips. "Ah, getting ready for bed?"

"Full marks for the lady," he said in a husky voice. Damn if this striptease wasn't winding him tighter than a spring. "Thought we might use some of those condoms you won."

"Condoms?" Emma cast a nervous glance at his erect cock then at the box full of condoms. She plucked a bright orange packet from the box and waved it in the air. "Do they make them big enough to cover you?"

"It will fit with no problem." He came to a halt in front of her.

She eyed his cock with misgiving, staring so hard he twitched.

"But will you fit?" she blurted.

For the first time in longer than he could remember, Jack wanted to laugh about sex. Grinning, he leaned over and cupped her face in his hands. "I promise that by the time I've finished with you we'll fit perfectly."

Emma had no idea what made Jack change his mind. He'd refused her earlier advances, but she wasn't about to object now that he was naked and sporting an impressive hard-on. She'd fantasized about this moment for months. Heck, at least a year.

She stood, ready to unzip her dress and shimmy free in case he changed his mind. If he displayed a hint of indecision, she'd jump him.

"Wait."

Emma froze, every muscle tensed to spring. Wait, as in stop, he didn't want to do this? She lifted her head, trying to read his expression. Yeah, right. A book with blank pages contained more information.

"I want to undress you."

"Oh." Emma nibbled her bottom lip while she considered this development then gave a decisive nod. He might as well see all of her straight off. Her body wasn't catwalk-model material, but with her height she'd look stupid with tiny bones and no padding. Emma hated pretense. "All right."

"With the light on," he added with distinct challenge.

In answer, Emma turned her back to present the zipper of her little black dress. Her heart raced while she waited for the first step in her master plan to commence. She wanted to grab. She wanted to touch the dragon tattoo on his biceps to discover if it was still hot to the touch. She wanted to kiss and fondle. But she did none of these things in case he backpedaled and changed his mind.

The zipper whined downward. No fumbling or cursing, just masculine competence that boded well for the actual act. The black fabric slithered downward and caught on her hips until he maneuvered the material safely over the obstruction. Before Emma could move, he swung her off her feet and dropped her on the bed. She hadn't even stopped bouncing when he was on her, pressing her into the mattress.

"You need to wear more clothes," he muttered, running his hands around her naked breasts.

"Frightened I'll catch cold?" God, his hands felt good on her bare skin, his abrasive touch intoxicating.

"I'm going to wonder each time I see you." He plucked at one nipple, hard enough that it should have hurt. Instead, the sensation traveled straight to her achy clit. Emma arched her back, silently pleading for him to do it again. "Think about your lingerie or lack of underwear."

Instead of repeating the nipple tweak, he kissed a trail across her rib cage, pausing to circle his tongue around her belly button. Emma groaned, a sudden mass of writhing nerves. He could do whatever he wanted when each caress went straight to her head—each stroke powerful and invigorating. The only thing that might feel better, well, she'd exert her rights to explore him later.

"No bra," he whispered, his warmth breath feathering across her lower belly. "Panties so brief I don't know why you bothered." His tongue traced the lacy elastic band that held her panties in place, across her lower abdomen then from her hip to inner thigh. "And then there's the stockings. Fuck, they're hot."

"I...um." She was dying here, so close to losing her cool. She stirred restlessly, the urge to beg him to rip off her panties and lick her, trembling on the tip of her tongue.

As if he'd read her mind, Jack tugged them down her legs, but left the thigh-high stockings where they were. His fingers felt callused on her legs and feet, even through the sheer stockings, as he edged the lacy material away. He reared up to a kneeling position beside her, parted her legs and looked his fill.

"Yeah," he murmured. "Don't move an inch. So pretty." He skimmed a finger across her labia.

Emma felt the flush of arousal that swept from her head to the tips of her pink toes. She felt wanton. She felt beautiful and feminine. And she wanted him desperately.

He grabbed a fistful of condoms from the box that still lay on the corner of the bed and dumped them on the wooden bedside cabinet before dropping the rest on the floor near the head of the bed. The plastic wrapping crackled as he opened the packet. Emma watched with fascination as he rolled the bright orange condom onto his penis. She licked her lips and fought the urge to fidget even as moisture gathered between her legs. He hadn't done much more than finger her and she was a quivering mass of desire.

Jack's hand slid in a long, luxurious stroke down her chest and over her belly, a trail of acute awareness prickling in his wake. A quick inhalation did nothing to counteract her sudden breathlessness. She swallowed, praying her heart didn't flutter right out of her chest as he drew a finger along her dew-slick cleft. He paused to circle her clit, and Emma started, the zing of excitement almost too much to bear. *Jeesh.* Was there such a thing as female premature orgasm? Because if she wasn't careful, it was going to happen to her. A tremor took her, and she strained upward to gain more pressure, her gaze darting to his impassive expression. Why was the man dithering? Did he want a diagram? A set of instructions?

"You're wet for me," he murmured.

Well, duh. That was obvious. No point in denying she wanted him. "Yes, of course."

He parted her legs even farther and moved into the space between. "But not wet enough. Can't wait any longer," he muttered almost to himself. Taking his cock in one hand, he rubbed it across the mouth of her pussy, coating the tip of his shaft in her juices.

Her mouth dried, her senses working overtime. His scent filled each quick breath. His touch fueled her desire. The choppiness of her breathing was almost deafening. With a pounding heart, she registered everything and craved even more.

Reaching over her, he grabbed a container of lubricant from the box. He broke the seal and pumped the bottle several times until a colorless gel squirted into the palm of his hand. With a soft grunt, he smoothed the gel in rough strokes along her cleft. Coolness hit her first, tickling and bringing a yelp, laughter, then warmth, intense and pleasurable as the lubricant coated her clitoris and pussy. Jack smoothed the excess along his erection. He probed her cleft, igniting nerve-endings until her breath caught. One finger slide into her channel, and she swallowed a whimper.

Way better than her imagination.

She groaned as he leisurely pumped two fingers inside her, stretching and preparing her for his entry.

"Better," he muttered as he pushed them inside her for a third time and slowly withdrew. He replaced his fingers with the thick head of his cock and filled her aching flesh. His growl echoed against the walls.

Emma bit her lip, wanting to make an appreciative noise too. Instead, she remained silent, not wanting to distract him or have him rethink his actions. One could never tell how Jack would react. While it made him a great detective, his unpredictability created difficulties in wooing him to her way of thinking.

Desire kicked hard as he pushed his cock deeper. Not much in the way of foreplay, but this time it was okay. Already an orgasm shimmered, just out of reach. She felt stretched, and still Jack kept up the pressure, thrusting and retreating until he was fully seated.

"You okay?" Jack's glower was downright scary.

Too bad. She was enjoying the experience, she thought dreamily, fit to bursting with happiness. It could only get better when her orgasm hit. "Yeah," she said in understatement. "I'm fine."

"Good." He upped the pace, thrusting and withdrawing in a steady, powerful rhythm that made the bed creak.

So good. Her mind hazed with pleasure as she rose to meet each thrust. Her pussy was on fire. *So close to exploding.* His hands traveled up to cup her breasts, then he flicked his thumbs over sensitive nipples. Emma moaned. He squeezed one distended nipple between finger and thumb, timing the pinch to coincide with an unhurried thrust into her pussy. The sharp nip sent frissons of pleasure skipping along her veins.

"Jack." She scarcely recognized her voice. The sensations built higher and higher, and she clung to his broad shoulders, arching her back and meeting each hard shove with a swivel of her hips.

Deep shudders shook the strong shoulders beneath her clinging hands. Each successive drive into her pussy moved Emma up the bed until her head banged against the padded headboard. Jack withdrew again and slammed home. She burned for fulfillment. *Burned.* Another push into her. Then the next thrust sent her over the edge into a world where sensation ruled. She cried out, riding the wave and wringing out every particle of pleasure.

Jack plunged into her once more and froze. Deep inside, Emma felt the pulse of his cock as semen jetted from him. His arms wrapped around her tight, tucking her firmly against his chest.

He sighed, right near her ear. "You okay?"

"Oh, yeah." Emma brushed a lock of hair off his forehead, then gave into temptation and traced his mouth with the tip of one finger. "What's next?"

Jack snorted a sound that might have been a laugh. She wasn't sure since she had trouble reading him, which was a damn shame since he was a mystery she was desperate to solve.

CHAPTER 4

Like any good private dick, Emma started her investigation in small increments and proceeded with caution. She wriggled from beneath Jack, taking him by surprise when she pushed him flat on the mattress. He blinked at her, and she hid her anticipation behind a small smile. Before she enticed him to play, she intended to explore every inch of his sexy body. No way was she leaving Mahoney Resort without trying out the toys and sex games she'd won.

Jack shifted away enough to remove the condom and discard it. He opened his mouth and looked as if he would order her to stop. Not gonna happen.

Distraction.

She needed one.

Now.

Emma bent and grazed her teeth over one flat nipple. She plucked at his other one with her fingers in the same manner she'd enjoyed him doing to her. Leaning closer, she slid her mouth across his flesh, tasting salt and smelling a hint of soap. Heady. Addicting. Very yummy. Her busy hands cupped his shoulders and explored farther afield, delighting in each new discovery—firm abs, bulging biceps, the mysterious dragon tattoo, flat belly and an erection that leapt beneath her questing fingers.

A huge, pulsing cock. She ran her fingers along the silky skin, feeling the inherent strength beneath. It was hidden in the same way an iceberg lurked beneath the surface of the ocean.

Jack was an iceberg.

He kept a tight lid on his emotions, never letting anyone close enough to glimpse his true thoughts. A challenge. He made a woman want to explore, to discover what made him tick.

Emma strummed her fingers along the underside of his cock. For the first time in her life, she wanted to try oral sex. She wanted to hold him in her mouth. Taste him.

A growl rumbled in his chest, but instead of alarm or fear, exhilaration swept to the fore. She lowered her head, the desire to experiment, a siren dance through her veins. She cupped his balls in her hands, squeezed gently then licked the length of his cock from base to tip.

Jack groaned, a dark, needy sound, his hands rising to tangle in her hair. Encouraged, Emma opened her mouth and took the very tip of him between her lips. She swiped her tongue over the slit at the end and a salty taste exploded across her taste buds. His hips jerked, thrusting upward in demand, and an incredible sensation of power suffused her.

He liked what she was doing.

With renewed confidence, she relaxed her jaw, opened her mouth wider and took more of him. Jack thrust again, with more control this time, yet still a silent command. She swirled her tongue and sucked, drawing on his cock—something delectable and delicious to savor.

"You can be a bit rougher." His husky voice brought a shiver, a frisking of her pleasure points. "But don't bite," he added when she opened her mouth wider still and introduced the slightest scrape of teeth.

She smirked, or as much as she could with a mouthful of cock. Desire roared to life—a thrill at the way he massaged her head with his big hands, at being the center of his focus.

He set up an easy surge and withdrawal, each successive thrust going deeper. His cock had been big before but now it filled her mouth and she loved it. Her breasts ached, swollen and needy of his caresses. A simmering sensation, half pain and half pleasure tortured her and made her hips writhe. Empty. She craved him. Juices moistened her folds. So wet. So desperate for his cock to fill the emptiness.

He pulled from her mouth without warning, taking her by surprise. "Did I do something wrong?"

Jack barked a laugh. "Hell no! Any more right now and I'll explode. I'd rather come inside your pussy." He levered up on his elbows to grab a condom off the bedside cabinet.

"I want to put it on." Emma held out her hand.

"Not this time." He ripped open the packet with his teeth and rapidly rolled the condom onto his shaft. "Ride me," he ordered, his dark eyes gleaming with promise.

"Oh, a challenge, huh?" Emma straddled his hips and grasped his cock. She couldn't resist stroking his length and feeling the power of him.

"Don't torture me, Emma. Or I'll take matters into my own hands."

Humor surfaced like a leaping dolphin. She was so tempted, but his fingers locked around her forearms in a silent bid for obedience. She positioned his cock and eased down, closing her eyes to savor the stretching of internal muscles, the slide of their bodies as they joined and he forged deeper.

"Move faster," he directed.

Emma snorted and executed a smart salute. "My ride. My way." She maintained her easy pace, enjoying the delicate sparks igniting her flesh.

He reached up to cup her breasts and tweaked one nipple. She gasped and caught her bottom lip between her teeth as a buzz roared through her sensitized body. After their earlier bout he knew she enjoyed the hint of roughness, but it still amazed her how the concept of pain—the rough tugs, the pinches—made her senses sizzle. Weird but fantastic.

His brown eyes glowed as he reached up to where their bodies joined and ran a teasing finger around her swollen clitoris. His touch was firm, but not enough to push her into orgasm.

"Please," Emma pleaded. "Do that again. A fraction harder. Now."

Jack grunted as she rose and lowered herself on his cock. Excruciatingly slow, for maximum enjoyment. "You want to give instruction but not to take it?"

"Ohhhh," Emma moaned. She swayed above him, feeling Herculean yet ravenous, feeling as though she could do anything if only her hunger for him was appeased. The first tremors of orgasm shimmered to life, radiating outward until fiery sparks licked her nerve endings. Her eyes drifted closed to savor the experience. The rise and the slow return. The sense of fullness. The slide of their bodies, the intimacy of their joining.

The shimmer deepened.

She sucked in a pained breath as she balanced on a precipice, unsure of whether to move again and push over or to remain poised in anticipation. Then she felt Jack's fingers, nimble and skilled, rubbing her in just the right place, just the right way.

A cry of pleasure escaped. Her pleasure. Her body jerked,

and she shattered. Her pussy clenched tight around Jack's cock. Emma's head tipped back as she rode out the exquisite bliss and slowly relaxed.

"My turn, princess," Jack whispered, and he gripped her hips and lifted her off him. Before she could blink, he'd placed her facedown on the bed and raised her arse in the air. His big hands cupped her buttocks, making her shiver with renewed awareness, despite the fleeting thought he was looking at her butt.

He could have as many turns as he wanted.

She wasn't finished with him yet.

Jack palmed her ass then ran a finger down the crevice between her butt cheeks. A tremor racked her and he hesitated. Despite his initial reluctance, he'd hate to frighten her. When she didn't voice an objection, he continued. Gripping his cock in one hand, he positioned himself at the mouth of her pussy. He pushed inside until her heat enveloped his shaft. She was wet—her juices coated his cock and made his surge and retreat easy and incredibly arousing.

But he needed more for what he intended. Jack reached for the lubrication again. Half of him expected questions, but they didn't come. Instead, she made a sexy moan that tightened his balls and made his blood run hotter. Who'd have guessed the little sparrow was such a sexual creature?

Jack pumped a generous amount of lube on his palm and

smeared it from where they were joined all the way up to the puckered rosette of her anus.

The dragon inside him roared. *Sex. Now.*

Jack held the beast back by setting up a lazy shuttle in and out of her pussy. His cock swelled as the pleasure assaulted him.

"What are you doing to me?" she whispered, her words throaty. Sexy.

Jack rubbed his finger back and forth over her rosette, delicately probing while continuing the steady strokes into her pussy. "Don't like it? Tell me to stop if I cross one of your lines."

"It feels different," Emma said finally. "But good. It's fine."

Jack made a mental note to check out the other sex toys. If she liked this and wanted to test her boundaries, he was ready.

The single light that shone over the bed highlighted her creamy skin. Being able to see his cock travel in and out of her was an incredible turn-on. His darker skin against her pale curves. Jack hastened the pace, removing his finger from her anus so he could grip her hips and hold her steady for each drive. He felt her quiver, the tiny clasps and clenches around his cock, and a growl of triumph vibrated low in his throat. He jerked his hips, ramming his cock home, flesh slapping flesh until he erupted, spurting his seed deep and hard, a harsh groan ripping free.

Gradually, he eased from Emma, separating their bodies. A sharp intake of breath made him still. The noise came from behind the mirror. Fuck, he'd forgotten their watchers. He'd forgotten everything except Emma and how it felt to pound into her sexy body. Admitting that fact, even to himself, scared the shit out of him.

"We need to check out all the different activities more closely," Jack informed her the next morning while trying to avoid glancing at Emma's cleavage and force away the memories of what they'd done to each other throughout the night. His testy dragon wasn't cooperating, stretching beneath his skin and demanding another hot and heavy session. His dick leaped with enough vigor to fuck a netball team—the whole seven plus the reserves. Bloody blue moon was really pushing his libido.

Emma dropped her hairbrush into her pink bag and rose from the stool that sat in front of the dressing table. "Good. Where do we go first?"

Jack ripped his gaze away and glared at the mirror above the bar. That was another thing. He couldn't be sure if a sound system went along with the two-way mirror. They'd have to watch what they discussed in case it was recorded.

He risked another glance. Emma's smile was so bright it almost blinded him.

Damn, now she had expectations.

He'd have to make it clear his lone status would never change. His attitude to the female sex would hurt her, and despite the necessity, he regretted the fact. Emma was a likable girl. Easy to spend time with and tempting. So bloody tempting. But after Rachel, he refused to step into another emotional wringer. Admitting to the taniwha monster thing, and the garbage that came along with the truth.

About him.

About George Taniwha Investigators and Security, and the team of taniwhas who worked as private investigators.

Nah, he'd skip the emotional crap. Better she was hurt a little now, than come face-to-face with monsters later.

"I think we should split up," he said in an undertone.

"Oh." She wrinkled her nose. "I thought we'd spend time together like the other couples."

"We have the week to do that." Jack scowled at the reminder of the mission constraint. It was tighter than Emma realized. With the blue moon on Saturday, he'd need plentiful sex or he'd have to shift to avoid excruciating pain. He'd hoped to have this case wrapped up fast so he could return home for the fall of the blue moon.

It was bloody inconvenient, but once he shifted, he was stuck in his taniwha form for twenty-four hours. Suffering through a full moon was bad enough but a blue moon...

Jack forced away the dire thoughts to concentrate on Emma. "I forgot to tell you. I made an appointment for you at the spa for this afternoon." He pulled a small card from his pocket and handed it to her.

Emma beamed. "Wow! Thank you."

"It's not all luxury." He leaned closer to whisper in her ear. "You need to ask questions and check out the spa area without causing suspicion. Think you can do that?"

She gave a decisive nod, although a frown creased her forehead as she said in a low voice, "I've trained for fact gathering. Which areas do you want me to check out this morning? Will we meet up for lunch? It might look a bit strange if we don't."

"Let's go. We'll talk on the way."

The early morning sun peeked over the stand of native trees, warming the clearing and petanque pit not far from the entrance to their apartment block.

Jack took Emma's arm and set a brisk pace. "We'll walk along the beach."

Emma tucked her hand into his as soon as the path widened enough for them to walk side by side. Jack froze momentarily before resuming his long strides to the beach. Her floral scent pulled at him, making it difficult to concentrate. Why did she have to touch him all the time? If she stroked her hand across his dragon tatt one more time...

"We need to watch what we say or discuss." Jack couldn't make up his mind whether to snatch his hand from her grasp or not.

Her touch burned, bringing every one of his senses to roaring life. He heard her soft breathing, the waves rushing to shore and a gull wheeling overhead, felt the soft texture of her hand and bare arm. Hell, he had to get a grip. *Concentrate.* "It's possible our room is bugged."

"Someone listening in on us? I wondered why...I don't—Someone's watching us right now! No, don't look." Emma leaned closer and twined her arms around his neck. "Kiss me."

It was an order, and Jack found himself in a lip-lock before he could voice questions. Her lips were soft, smooth and moist and distracting. She slipped her tongue between his lips, and he was a goner. Taste and sensation kicked him in the gut, combining with the feel of her curvy breasts plastered against his chest. His taniwha gave a sleepy yawn then woke rapidly with a demanding growl.

Jack took over the kiss, plunging his tongue into her mouth and withdrawing in a facsimile of the sexual act. Suddenly, he wanted to rip her clothes off and plunge into her hot pussy. He didn't care about an audience or the public location. He just wanted to fuck her senseless. But what he desired and what he received were two very different things. Jack struggled to hold on to the semblance of his remaining sanity.

Her fingers curled into his shoulders, her nails digging into his flesh through his thin shirt. The small pain jerked his cock tight enough to cause him discomfort. Emma wriggled even closer, rubbing against his chest and groin and making a sound resembling a purr. Dammit if his dragon didn't purr in tandem.

Jack tore his mouth from Emma's. Panic roared to life as the taniwha clamored inside his head, demanding he take what Emma offered. The ever-present guilt surfaced, bringing uneasiness in its wake. He was using her, and he had to stop because he didn't intend to give her what she needed—a happy future.

He removed his hands from her shoulder and back and took a giant step to separate them. She deserved a man who could commit wholly to her. He wasn't that man.

"I'm not doing that again," he said in a flat tone. "What's our watcher doing?"

"Nothing. I made it up." Emma lifted her chin with an air of hauteur. "There isn't anyone watching. This is a low-level investigation. George said so."

"Dammit, Emma. Our room is bugged." Frustration rode him hard. If she'd been a male, he could've punched her. He should inform her about the two-way mirror. If he could trust her to maintain natural behavior, he would've told her about the voyeurs.

He stared at the thin gold chain spanning her neck, his hands fisting. Taking a deep breath, he said, "This is the plan this morning. I'm going to check out the gym since that is the most logical place for drugs. I want you to reconnoiter the pool area and this afternoon the spa. Talk to people. Mahoney has to shift the drugs somehow."

Thankfully, Emma must have realized she'd pushed him hard

enough and remained silent.

"We'll meet for lunch and compare notes. Keep your hands to yourself. We're not having sex again. Last night was a mistake." Jack turned away from her wounded expression and stomped off without looking back.

Later that afternoon

Emma didn't understand Jack. He ran hot then cold like an unreliable water tap. It was difficult to keep up with his quirks. One minute, he seemed to enjoy kissing her and the sex...

She relaxed and conjured the memory of their bodies sliding together in the many different ways they'd tried the night before. The way his muscular body moved beneath her hands. His sexy dragon tatt.

A tingle sprang to life between her thighs and she stirred restlessly on the sheet-covered couch inside the spa. The idea of never making love with him again sent a touch of panic blasting through her. She had to get him to change his mind. And if he didn't, she'd try again. They were good together, and one time didn't qualify as a win in the bet with her girlfriends.

The slap of soft soles on the tiled floor heralded the return of the spa attendant. Emma lifted her head. Eek, that green stuff looked nasty. Didn't smell much better, either. Perhaps Jack had intended this spa visit as punishment.

The attendant smeared the green paste all over her back, from shoulders to toes and bade her lie still to let the stuff dry for five minutes. Then, Emma had to turn over for the woman to smear the paste on her front. Once she resembled the original green alien, she was left in solitary splendor to dry and absorb the sea weedy goodness. Mood music slipped stealthily from concealed speakers while the green glop did its work.

An hour later, the woman shook her awake and directed her to the shower. Feminine chatter hit her the second she opened the door into the huge shower block. In the outer area, large mirrors covered the wall. A line of padded stools stood ready for women to attend to makeup and hair. A vase of pink roses and white gypsophila fragranced the air.

Emma picked her way into the steam-filled shower area. Several women, with varying shades of paste covering their bodies, were waiting for showers.

Time for questions, Emma thought, remembering Jack's terse instructions. "Your paste doesn't smell much better than my seaweed."

The other woman laughed. "Ah, but I'm a prettier color."

"That's debatable." Emma studied the bright yellow decorating the other woman.

"Oh, look. The communal shower's emptying. Let's grab it.

We'll be waiting for ages for these ones."

Emma shrugged. Suited her. She grabbed the canvas bag the spa had provided for her clothes and hurried over to the communal shower with her new friend close on her heels. Three other women followed, each of them a different color, and covered head to toe with a similar thick paste.

"I don't know which of us looks worst." Emma glanced from woman to woman with a critical eye.

"I hope they don't have security cameras getting shots of my naked ass," a dark-haired woman said.

Emma blinked. "Do you think anyone will recognize it in purple?"

They glanced from one to the other then burst into shrieks of laughter.

"Last one to wash off is a rotten egg," one said.

"You already look like a rotten egg," Emma quipped.

As one, they made for the shower door with good-natured pushing, breasts and butts jostling amid lots of laughter.

Ten minutes later, they were clean and ready for the next part of their treatments.

"How about we meet up at the bar afterward?" the ex-purple woman suggested.

"Good idea," Emma said. It would give her a chance to ask questions. "I want to see how we all turn out," she added with a conspiratorial grin.

"Make it the poolside bar," another suggested, "and we can watch the sunset."

Two hours later, Emma walked into the poolside bar. She had no trouble spotting the women. Raising her hand in greeting, she ambled over to the bar and waited for the barman to finish with his current customer.

Her gaze wandered the proximity before settling back on the barman. With his blond surfer-boy looks, he was easy on the eye. His blue resort shirt stretched over muscular shoulders, the tight sleeves highlighting a set of well-developed biceps. Emma frowned.

"Would you like me to suggest a cocktail?" the barman asked in a husky voice. "Can't have a pretty lady getting frown lines."

Emma started and gave a self-conscious laugh. "I was miles away. What would you suggest?"

"How about the house special cocktail? Good for whatever ails you. Tastes good, too."

"Sure." Emma watched his deft movements as he sliced an orange. "Do you enjoy working here? Are you allowed to use the facilities on your days off?"

"I use the gym," the barman said as he competently measured and mixed a cocktail for her. "The job suits me. Everyone's happy. Lots of people wanting fun."

Women throwing themselves at him, she translated as she intercepted the avid gaze of an attractive brunette at the other end of the bar. "Maybe you can give me some quick advice—if you do weights that is."

"I enter Ironman contests. I've lifted my share of weights."

"What's your name? Have you placed in any of the local competitions?"

"I came second in the Taupo Ironman."

Emma oohed and ahhed and fluttered her lashes. She leaned over the bar to stroke her fingers across his forearm. "Wonderful. If I wanted to train for a bodybuilding contest, who should I talk to at the gym? Just for some initial pointers. I've been thinking about it for a long time now. No time like the present."

"Max is the one you need to see," the barman said without hesitation. "He's an ex-bodybuilder and knows everything that's worth knowing."

"Thanks. I'll check it out first thing tomorrow morning. Nice to chat with you." She paid for her cocktail and wandered over to the group of women by the pool.

"Hello." Emma pulled out a chair and sat.

"We're going to play strip poker. Want to join us?"

Emma hesitated before deciding it would be a good opportunity to get to know the women. It was possible one of them had info or had seen something to help in their investigation. She'd slip her questions into the general conversation. "Okay, but you'll have to show me how to play."

"Oh, good." One of the women rubbed her hands together and grinned wickedly. "A rookie to fleece. Deal up."

Jack checked their accommodation, but Emma wasn't there. Since he couldn't hear any vibrations from behind the mirror, he took the opportunity to search for surveillance equipment. If there were hidden cameras, his search would alert those who'd rigged their room, but he decided to risk detection.

Instinct told him the cameras were activated whenever the voyeurs were present to prevent the need to search hours of meaningless film for the good stuff. They were probably able to guess times when the occupants were present since most guests would attend the gala dinners and special nights. Either that, or they had resort staff alert them once guests entered their rooms.

He moved around the walls in a systematic manner, searching every conceivable hiding place for audio and video devices.

Finding nothing, he checked his watch. Perhaps it was as he'd thought—they'd lucked out scoring a room for voyeurs to access, making the addition of sound unnecessary. Or, they'd decided it would be easier to add a soundtrack later, something with more appeal for their audiences than the words of an innocent actor.

He paused and grimaced. Nah, couldn't be that simple. Surely, they'd want sound? Jack crossed to the bed and sat while he considered the problem. Where the hell could they hide sound equipment? Enlightenment hit, along with a feral grin of triumph. Under the bloody bed.

Bingo, he thought less than a minute after his brainwave. The equipment wasn't recording at present, which backed up his supposition about their recording times. They didn't want to waste film. He tugged at the wiring in such a way that it appeared as if the resort staff had damaged it while vacuuming under the bed. He'd check each time they returned. It should be simple enough now he knew the location of the equipment.

He wandered over to the window and stared out at the sea view. Should Emma's absence concern him?

Outside, the sun was starting to set. Ribbons of fiery red and orange spread across the horizon as the sun sank lower. Over on the mainland, people started to switch on their lights and they twinkled in pockets of illumination along the coast.

Jack paced the length of the bedroom and back. Time for a drink. Tension whitened his knuckles, and he didn't have to think too hard to analyze the cause. *Emma*. He checked his watch again before deciding to shower and change for the themed pirate dinner.

Half an hour later, Jack was ready, dressed in tight black trousers and a loose white shirt that made him feel like a sissy. Tight black leather boots encased his feet and calves. He caught a glimpse of his reflection in the mirror and snorted. A Māori buccaneer. He'd be glad when this assignment ended and his life reverted to normal.

Meanwhile, he was *really* looking forward to the tarts and vicars night later in the week.

What the devil was Emma doing? Although they hadn't agreed on a meeting time, he'd implied it would be before dinner. In his mind at least. He grabbed the keycard, thrust it inside his back trouser pocket and slammed outside. If something had happened to her, he'd never forgive himself. And if she didn't have an excellent reason for not showing up and worrying him, he'd wring her bloody neck.

The bar near the restaurant was hopping, full of pirates ready to plunder and party the night away. Emma wasn't there. A few people had drifted into the restaurant and the reception area, but still no sign of her.

The pool bar wasn't as busy, but there was a cluster of people, mainly men, at the far end of the outdoor balcony. Despite the warmth of the evening, a gas heater burned above the table where the group sat. Roars of laughter filled the air followed by the odd groan.

"Come on, Emma," a male voice chided loudly. "Concentrate."

Jack's gut tightened as he strode to the massed group.

"Forget what he told you, love." The voice was low and slurred. "Don't concentrate. Get your gear off. Show us your pussy."

Jack elbowed his way through the men crowding around the table.

A tall, thin office-worker type snapped, "What do you think

you're doing?"

Jack cast him a ferocious glare and affronted office-guy backed up, now in alarm-mode. Wise man. Jack took one look and cursed.

Fuck, he was gonna wring her neck. His hands flexed at the pleasurable thought as he scanned her flushed face. The woman was tipsy, giggling fit to wake the dead, and practically naked. His gaze tracked over her butt, and he corrected himself. She was naked. Those panties didn't cover enough to call her clothed.

He stepped up behind her naked back and bent to breathe in her ear. "What are you doing?"

Emma whirled so quickly her naked breasts jiggled. "Losing," she warbled.

Alcoholic fumes hit him in the face. "I can see that," Jack said with a calm he didn't feel.

The four women sitting around the same table were in various stages of undress but wore more clothes than Emma. Jack wanted to grab a towel, a tablecloth, anything to cover her beautiful breasts. All of a sudden, he felt possessive. He hated the other men seeing the tiny mole on the curve of her left breast. And if the guy behind him didn't stop pushing in order to cop an eyeful of Emma and her semi-clothed friends, Jack intended to rearrange his nose. The beefy male could have fries with the busted nose if he wanted—Jack wasn't fussy.

Emma turned and beckoned him closer. She wrapped her arms around his neck and whispered in his ear. "I don't want to lose. I hate to lose, but I don't know what to do with my hand. Can you help me?"

"Yeah, okay. What have you got in your hand?"

Emma fanned out her cards so he could see. Feeling the weight of a stare, Jack glanced up. Every one of the four women sitting at the table was staring at him. Suddenly, Jack felt like a lump of beef dangled in front of a pack of wolves. He turned away to concentrate on Emma's cards. She had a pair of sixes and that was it. He fought for an impassive face while cursing a storm to his taniwha. With that hand, she was screwed. Unless she bluffed. Jack leaned closer to whisper instructions in her ear. She turned to him and winked.

Surprise kicked him in the ribs. She wasn't as drunk as she seemed.

"Are you in?" the dark-haired woman who was dealing asked.

Emma's body language screamed confident, and pride grew in Jack. "I'm in."

"Cards?" the dealer asked.

Emma didn't bother to look at her cards before she shook her head.

"I'll take two," one woman said.

The men crowding the table were silent as they watch the ending stages of the game. Jack scanned the faces, ready to lash out if anyone tried to help by letting the others know Emma was bluffing.

"I fold."

"Me too."

"I'm out." The cards slapped on the table.

The last woman studied Emma then laid down her cards. "I'm out."

"Take it off! Take it off!" The chant started with one burly jackass and others joined in as the four women removed a garment each.

Jack noticed gooseflesh forming on Emma and decided to take action. "Sorry to be a spoilsport, but I need Emma to come with me. Maybe you can finish the game tomorrow?" *Over his dead body.*

"Good," said the slim blonde sitting on Emma's right. "I'm getting cold, and I'm also chicken." She laughed, gesturing at her pale pink panties. They were her sole remaining item of clothing. "I have a premonition I'm going to be the first one naked. I'm quitting while I'm ahead."

Jack relaxed as the men started to drift away. "Ladies." He inclined his head and turned to Emma. "Ready?"

Emma sensed he wasn't pleased with her. It was in the set of his shoulders and the grim line of his mouth. Well, he could just deal. She had flushed out a few leads to check tomorrow, and she wasn't going to apologize for her methods. Besides, she wasn't the only one to bare her breasts tonight.

"It won't take me long to get ready. I'll meet you back here."

Jack handed Emma her T-shirt, his dark eyes glinting dangerously. "I don't think so."

Damn, he was going to be difficult.

Emma pulled the shirt over her head and stepped into her denim shorts. She picked up her shoes, dropped them inside the canvas bag the spa had allowed her to keep and stalked toward their room. Jack fell into step behind her.

The walk back took forever. Emma was very conscious of Jack's presence. She could feel his glare between her shoulder blades but that didn't stop her adding an extra sway to her hips. Her nipples were already pulled tight from the chill of the night air, but now they tingled. She sucked in a hasty breath and hustled. The path changed from pavement to gravel, and she winced at the sharp stones beneath the soles of her feet.

"What's wrong?" The tone was sharp enough to warn her he was on the edge of an explosion. Time to cease the teasing—for today at any rate.

"Bare feet," she muttered.

Without warning, he swept her up and dangled her over his shoulder. Her butt poked into the air and blood rushed to her head. Her canvas bag hit his arse with each step.

"What are you doing?" she shrieked, kicking ineffectually with her feet. "My brains will fall out."

"Close your mouth and you won't lose them," he snapped, tightening his grip on her flailing limbs. He strode along the graveled path without difficulty or a hint of labored breathing.

Emma took a deep breath, ready to harangue him, when she glanced toward the ground. Her gaze lit on his butt. It was tightly encased in black trousers. A spectacular view. She wanted to bite. Really badly. She licked her lips and suddenly being so close to Jack wasn't an undignified punishment. It was a gift. Her heart pounded as he stalked through the automatic doors at the entrance to their accommodation block. Between her legs moistened with her carnal thoughts, truly wicked ones that circled her mind like a bird of prey hunting for an evening meal.

"Quit that," Jack barked as he paused to pluck the keycard from his pocket. He shouldered open the door and negotiated the entrance without hurting her. Then, he let her slide back over his shoulder until her feet hit the ground. The brush of her unbound breasts against his shoulder and hard chest made her gasp. The intimate touch of his hand on her arse as he helped her stand made her gulp.

"Quit what," she whispered.

"Those little sighs." He retreated as if she'd scalded him. His dark eyes held wariness as they moved over her face and flickered down her length.

She barely suppressed her shiver of desire.

Jack could smell her arousal, and it woke his dragon, the part he was desperately trying to keep in lockdown. The beast roared his need for sex. Hot, sweaty, uninhibited sex. Then, she ambled toward him, her hips swaying with a pert wiggle that made his throat tighten along with every appendage on his body. When he felt the wall at his back, he realized he'd been in a steady retreat. Now, the only way to avoid Emma was to move her out of the way, which would involve physical contact.

She touched him first, and he couldn't restrain his flinch. Her finger pads were hot, the heat searing through his thin shirt and into his skin beneath.

"You enjoy my sighs." Her voice was low. Breathy. And she made him think of sex even more. His cock was painfully tight, nudging against the placket of his trousers.

"No." Damn, the one night had been bad enough. Another... His conscience groaned and spoke sternly. *Don't. Do. It.*

"You're trembling."

Him? He didn't...shit! He was shaking like a tree in a storm. "Shouldn't you get ready for the pirate dinner?" *Feeble, Jack. Real feeble. Exert yourself, man. Act like her boss instead of a victim.* She moistened her lips until they gleamed in the moonlight, sidetracking him.

"I don't feel like going to the dinner. I'm tired." He caught her glance at the bed with a sense of alarm. With that come-hither expression, no way did she have intentions of resting or sleep.

CHAPTER 5

The woman was undressing him with her eyes. Jack felt the situation escalating from his control, and with his taniwha's roars resounding in his mind, his grip was tenuous at best. Then, she raised a hand and traced the V of flesh visible at his neck.

One tiny touch and he lost all restraint. He grabbed her by the shoulders and yanked her against his chest. Fuck, her soft curves pillowed him, fitting as precisely as his prized army boots. So good. She leaned her weight against him, brushing her belly against his cock. His cursed trousers had grown so tight Jack wondered if he'd lose circulation to his groin.

The horrible thought faded once their lips collided, greedy and ravenous for a taste of each other. He explored her mouth, the contrasting hardness of her teeth and the softness inside her cheek.

She tasted of limes and salt. Emma. It was damn addictive. When they finally parted, they were both breathing hard.

A soft smile played on her lips. "Did you want to go to the dinner?"

"No." But he didn't want this either. Another night of horizontal dancing with Emma smacked of heading down Commitment Road. Just a hop, skip and a dance away from Wedding Row.

His hands tightened around her shoulders. Nope, not a good idea. He'd push her away. Push her away—

Liar.

Jack wanted sex with Emma so badly his body still trembled. Even the idea of voyeurs didn't bother him as much as it had at the start.

Her warm hands burrowed under the fabric of his shirt, and just like that, Jack's willpower toppled, and he gave up the fight. "Dammit, woman. You're killing me here. If you're going to undo things, start with the trousers. They're cutting off my circulation."

"Poor baby," she cooed. "Can't have that." She redirected nimble fingers to his fly and cupped his erection, teasing him some more.

Jack heard her wildly beating pulse and knew she was excited. "I bet your panties are wet. I bet you're wet for me."

A soft blush suffused her cheeks. "Why don't you find out?" she whispered, her lashes drifting downward to hide the sleepy expression in her blue eyes.

With a reluctant grin, he slid his hands beneath the hem of her T-shirt. Blue. It matched her eyes. His fingers skimmed the warm flesh of her belly. She sucked in a rapid breath and her stomach as well. He ignored the feminine vanity. To his mind, she was perfect. He didn't suffer from a sore neck when he kissed her, and there was no danger of flattening her in a missionary position.

Yeah, she was perfect—more's the pity.

His fingers traced across her rib cage then a little higher to hold the generous weight of one plump breast. He lifted her T-shirt, exposing her breasts to his gaze.

"Beautiful." Jack wet his forefinger in his mouth and traced around the areola of one breast. Her pink nipple puckered, drawing tighter before his fascinated gaze. Leaning closer, he blew, his breath warm.

Emma shuddered and made a tiny sound of encouragement at the back of her throat. Jack had never taken the time to explore a feminine body in this detail. Had never been interested in anything but satiating his taniwha's demands. But now, despite the insistent pain in his groin, he wanted to stroke and pet, to explore the mysteries of Emma. He pressed a kiss in the valley between her breasts and licked along the fine web of blue veins beneath the pale surface. Strawberries. Tonight, she smelled of sweet, juicy strawberries.

"Stop teasing me," she said in a thick demand.

"I want to make sure I win my bet. I want you wet—dripping with your juices—so I can pound between your legs the minute I remove your panties."

Another shudder racked Emma. Jack smiled against the curve of her breast and placed tiny kisses, tantalizingly brief on her plump flesh, near her nipple and on the undersides of the weighty globes.

Emma tangled her hands in his hair, gripping tightly as she tried to direct his mouth to her nipple. Her fingernails dug into his scalp, and his amusement deepened.

"Hurry," she said with a grumpy edge to her voice.

Instead of giving her the relief she wanted, Jack let his hands drop to the dome snap at the waistband of her shorts. He tugged the fastening and it parted with a sharp crack. The zipper slid down, allowing the denim material to sag around her hips. Jack wet his finger again and ran it along the elastic waistband of her panties. He studied the damp trail he'd left and sucked in a deep breath. Fuck. His cock ached, the pressure for release intense and unrelenting. But if he waited, held off, his orgasm would be mind-blowing. A memory to dig out once he returned to solitary life alone in his seaside home with only his scruffy tomcat for company.

Jack knelt in front of her, sliding the shorts down her long legs. He helped her balance so she could step out and kick them away.

The increased scent of her arousal hit him hard—spicy and seductive and with a hint of strawberry. The same fruity aroma that perfumed her skin. He pressed his nose against her lower belly and breathed her in so he would remember. His lips moved, and he scraped his teeth against the sensitive flesh, nipping then soothing.

"I'm hot for you now, Jack," she said almost defiantly.

"Let's see, shall we?" But even though his words indicated action, he still dallied, teasing both of them to the point of madness. He palmed her naked buttocks, gripping one cheek in each hand. More than a handful, just the way he liked—a sexy curve to hold on to when he wanted to thrust into her tight pussy. He kneaded the flesh, enjoying the fact she never attempted to hide her generous ass or try to wriggle away from his attentions. Jack liked that about Emma—the acceptance of her size.

He loosened his grip on one butt cheek and ran his fingers in the crevice between. Emma jumped in surprise as he followed the G-string down. Then she rocked her hips, trying to massage her clit to gain relief.

"Not yet, sweet cheeks." Jack allowed his finger to travel between her legs, just a brief foray. His finger emerged wet. Emma was ready for his possession. Jack tipped back his head to meet her gaze.

"Please," she murmured, shifting her weight from foot to foot.

He lifted the damp finger to his mouth and maintaining her gaze, licked it clean, savoring the tart taste of her juices. She moaned, her blue eyes dark with arousal.

"Would you like my mouth on you? We haven't done that yet."

Her nose wrinkled a fraction before she nodded.

Jack ran his fingers under the elastic band of her G-string and tugged away her panties.

There were changes from this morning. "What have you done?" he murmured, shaking his head. It seemed the spa had a lot to answer for. "What else did you do in that spa?"

Emma glanced at her pelvic region. "I thought my heart looked sexy. And besides, you made the appointment."

Well, he couldn't argue with that. "It's...cute." Jack stared at the close-clipped heart that shielded her femininity. He drew her panties down her legs and then leaned closer to lick around the edge of the heart. She smelled intoxicating, and he gave in to the temptation to comb his fingers through the heart then made a quick foray along her naked cleft. "You're not sore?"

"No side effects from the shaving. Not yet anyway. They gave me some cream in case I have itching. Are you going to take all night?"

"Just drawing out the anticipation." And making himself crazy with lust, but the wait would be worth it. He glanced at his hand and saw the glint of scales starting to form on the top of his hand. The shadow of claws had formed beneath his fingernails, ready to pop into webbed talons. He'd run out of time to play. "Turn around. Put your hands on the wall."

She hesitated, tugging her bottom lip between dainty white teeth.

"Do it."

Slowly, she turned to face the beige-colored wall but cast another doubtful glance over her shoulder.

"Hands against the wall."

Emma sucked in an audible breath, but she placed her hands, one at a time on the painted wall, her heartbeat double-timing and drawing his taniwha even closer to the surface.

Jack ripped at the laces that fastened his shirt at the neck.

"What are you doing?" Emma half turned.

"Look at the wall," he barked. Jack scrambled for an excuse to keep her from seeing his partial change. Iridescent scales shimmered on his chest—pearl-gray scales the same color as the inside of a mussel shell. Thank God, his chest always changed before his back. If he hurried, the change would recede. "We're doing a role-play and you're the submissive. That means you follow orders. For a change."

Please let her follow his directions. Jack eyed her still body with misgiving. He yanked at his belt buckle and peeled the trousers over his swollen cock with care. Seconds later, he kicked the trousers out of his way and grabbed a condom. His breathing sounded harsh to his ears, and his hands shook, suddenly clumsy, dexterity compromised by the start of his change to taniwha form. He unrolled the condom awkwardly onto his penis, hoping like hell he didn't put a hole in the rubber with the sharp claws that extended from his fingers. The last thing he needed were baby taniwhas running around Auckland.

"What does a submissive do?" she whispered, still thankfully staring at the wall.

"Follows orders," he growled. If Emma decided to disobey, he wasn't certain of his next actions. Maybe he should introduce a bit of kink. Keep her busy with new experiences. And definitely a blindfold because if he didn't make haste, it was going to take time for the scales to fade back into his skin. "A submissive does what they're told without questioning. I'm not sure you could manage."

"Of course I can," she snapped.

Jack grinned at her indignation. A sharp, nagging pain knifed him in the gut, making him fold forward in agony. Damn, if he didn't hurry, he'd land in trouble. He cast a belligerent gaze toward the window. The moon was almost full, and he could feel its siren pull with every particle of his body. Another sharp twinge made him grunt. Fuck, he hoped Emma was as ready for his possession as he thought, because he wouldn't manage gentle tonight.

Jack ambled up to Emma and gingerly ran his finger pads over the silky smooth skin of her back, taking care not to scratch her with his claws.

"Spread your legs farther apart," he whispered, hoping she wouldn't notice the changed timbre of his voice. Generally, his vocal cords changed slowly, allowing him to speak in a growl before he shifted. Once he changed, all he could do was grunt or roar.

Emma widened her stance, drawing his attention to the full cheeks of her ass. He stepped up behind her so the fronts of his thighs brushed the backs of her legs.

"You feel hot."

"I am." Jack curled his hand around his cock and brushed the tip across the soft flesh of her backside. The resulting jolt ran the length of his body. He changed the direction, massaging his tip down the crevice between her ass cheeks.

Jack fingered her, skimming his fingers across the sensitive nub nestled in her core.

"Ohhh," she whispered, shifting her weight slightly and pushing her arse outward.

The soft moan reverberated, and his lips quirked as he leaned closer to nip the sensitive cords of her neck. Emma was responsive with no pretenses. No secrets. Jack's hands snaked around to cup her breasts in his hands. Guilt rose but he shoved it aside. He had a job to do, and this was the best way to complete his mission.

"I'm wet for you now," she complained. "You must have noticed. *Ohhh!* Do that again."

A muscle jumped in his jaw and his cock swelled impossibly tight at her sexy sound. Jack kissed her shoulder again then sucked on her flesh. "You ready for me to fuck you?"

"Yesss," Emma hissed with a trace of impatience.

Jack felt the absurd need to hold himself in check, to savor this experience, but he already balanced on the line between pleasure and pain. He pumped his cock with one hand then pushed into her warmth. Fuck. So damn good. The feel of her—tight, clinging and grasping his dick so sweetly. Enough to send a man mad or keep a taniwha sane. God, she felt so good. Deep shudders shook him as he stroked, hard and fast into her heat.

Thank God, the change had slowed. His claws retracted a fraction. The closeness with Emma and the charged hormones running through him had pushed the dragon back to its den. Scales still glinted beneath his skin, but he could explain the phenomena away if necessary.

"More," Emma demanded. Although she'd been skeptical about him taking her against a wall, he'd made her so hot, so quickly she could barely think. All she could do was feel. Jack slid a hand over her belly and lower, to rub her clit. His cock filled her impossibly full, possessing her and stamping ownership. Frissons of excitement swelled to a heady spill of pleasure. Another pass of his finger pushed her over the edge and she shattered—a full body experience with fireworks of color flickering behind her eyelids. Her breaths came in harsh pants, echoed by a grunt as Jack pumped into her and held still, his cock expelling semen deep inside her.

She sighed as the ripples of pleasure kept coming, gentler now but still consuming. Already, she wanted another turn. Jack had her hooked, literally addicted, and she didn't think she'd ever manage to look at another man again.

He nuzzled her shoulder, his chest pressed against her back. He pulled out of her, removed the condom, and led her over to the bed. They stared at each other for a long moment. Jack looked away first, glancing at the mirror above the bar.

"Interested in trying out some of the toys you've won?" he asked.

"Yes, please." Happiness suffused Emma without warning. Sometimes, it seemed as if Jack was making love to her against his will. But if he wanted to play with toys, then it must be her imagination. She plucked her box of goodies off the bedside table and handed it to him. "What do you want to do first?"

She took pleasure in watching him as he studied the contents of the box. His face was in the dark, his hair tousled, making him look mysterious and sexy. She leaned closer, brushing her breasts against his dragon tattoo.

Jack chose two items from the box and handed them to her. A glowing thing that resembled a penis but had a sort of handle at the end. Emma read the packaging and felt hot all over. A butt plug. She'd liked it when Jack had touched her there before. Excitement rose inside at the thought of trying something new. The other was a jar of chocolate paste. Emma turned the package over to read the instructions. There were several illustrations of breasts decorated with the paste and made to resemble edible items. A snigger emerged. "Which one are we going to try?"

Jack grinned suddenly, making Emma catch her breath and stare. So sexy. She wanted to soak in the warmth and wallow in his attention. "I've always liked Christmas pudding," he murmured, reclaiming the package from her. He opened it, and the deep, rich scent of chocolate filled the air. Emma watched as he dipped his finger into the jar. He raised it to his lips and licked the paste away.

Desire unfurled in her belly. He pushed her back against the pillows and bent to take a nipple in his mouth. Jack drew hard. And just like that, Emma was hot and ready for another round. Needy. Desperate. Why play with toys when she had the real thing?

"Jack?"

He glanced up, his dark eyes glowing strangely. *A quirk of the light.* "I need you inside me," Emma said. "We have all night. We can play with toys later."

Maintaining her gaze, he set the jar aside and reached for a condom. He covered his erection with calm, confident moves. "Just a little chocolate," he murmured. "I want to taste it on your skin."

Emma shivered at the avid note in his voice. No doubt about it—she was gonna die a happy woman.

"You like Thai food, too?" Emma paused in the middle of applying suntan lotion, ready to hit the pool straight after breakfast. "There's a great Thai restaurant near Botany Downs. We should go out for dinner when we get back to Auckland."

"We're not a couple." The flat and final tone of his voice made Emma stare.

Shock punched her in the lungs, stealing her breath. "I thought—"

Jack scowled. "Emma. I'm a male, and I need sex. You're handy and willing. It's as simple as that."

Her mouth opened then snapped shut. Her jaw worked but words jammed in her throat. She swallowed once. Twice. After coughing, she managed to squeeze out a few words. "What you're saying is that our affair comes to an end once we leave the resort?"

Jack lifted his gaze toward the ceiling. "By George, I think she's got it."

"You bastard." The urge to wrap her hands around his neck and squeeze until he gasped for air struck so strongly she shook with the need. Tempting, but too quick. He needed to suffer. "I have—" She broke off mid-sentence. No way was she letting him trample her feelings more than he had already. Tears built but she fought the feminine weakness. She straightened her shoulders and forced herself to meet his gaze without a flinch. "Fine. At least I know where I stand. I won't force myself on you again." Although she tried to keep her voice even, the bite of temper colored it dark and gave her words weight.

Her canvas bag lay beside the bed. Averting her gaze from the ruffled bedcovers, she grabbed it in her left hand. "I'm going out."

"Where?"

He had no right to demand answers. Her hand fisted so hard, the canvas strap of the bag dug into her palm. "I'm going to breakfast. I missed dinner and I'm starving."

"Wait five minutes, and I'll come with you."

Emma stared at him incredulously. *Obtuse, thick head.* Did he want her to draw attention to them by having the mother of all temper tantrums in public? Because that was a dead cert—if he didn't quit with the big, bad private investigator act.

"I don't think so." Emma terminated the conversation by leaving and shutting the door quietly behind her.

She stomped along the passageway to the front entrance. Despite informing Jack of her intentions to go to breakfast, she headed straight for the gym to start some subtle questioning.

The quicker they solved the case, the sooner she could head home to lick her wounds. The thought gave her pause.

She'd failed in her mission.

Emma glared at the innocent gardener trimming shrubs and stormed down the path to the main part of the resort. Bypassing the restaurant, she continued to the gym.

A blond male, a few years younger than she, manned the reception desk. Highly tanned and muscled, he looked as if he belonged in a fitness ad for a magazine.

"Morning. Can I help you?"

Emma cast aside her sudden doubts. "I've never been to a gym before. I thought this week would be a good time to see if I'd like

97

it before I pay for a membership at home. How do I start?" She'd scope out the territory before she asked questions.

"How about a tour of the facilities? How does that sound?" The receptionist—his name badge read Allen—gave her his whole attention, making her feel important and soothing her wounded spirit.

Emma shook free of his charismatic spell and nodded. "That sounds perfect."

Allen picked up a phone, and minutes later, another employee who could have been Allen's twin joined them.

Emma was introduced to various machines and shown the aerobics area, the weights area, the indoor swimming pool where a vigorous water aerobics session was underway. Once again, the instructor was an Allen clone but with red hair this time.

"You all look very fit." Emma batted her eyelashes at her guide. She paused, hoping he'd pick up the conversation batten. If not, she'd play bimbo and ask stupid questions.

"Most of us are in training. Mahoney Resort enters a triathlon team in the Ironman competitions. I made the team," he added with modesty.

"That's awesome." She fluttered her lashes and peeked at him to judge the effect. Yes, he was lapping up her act. She let a tiny gurgle escape and flashed a grin. "What's a triathlon?"

"It's a competition. Competitors swim, they do a bike ride and then they have to run. Have you heard of Martin Hamilton? He won a gold medal at the Olympic games for New Zealand."

"That's cool," Emma cooed, closing the small gap between them. "Have you won a medal?"

"I'm going to one day," he said with confidence.

How? How did he know that? Or was he just psyching himself up? Positive thinking and all that? Emma thought rapidly, unsure of how hard to push. "Have you been training hard?" Her voice was breathless as she ran her fingers along his bulging biceps. The man was gorgeous with his grin and muscular physique, a real hottie, yet she didn't feel a thing.

He wasn't Jack.

Emma's mouth firmed at the thought. Jack didn't deserve her loyalty. And now she understood why he had a procession of babes waltzing through his life. Jack didn't want to commit. He was a coward.

Her guide frowned, and Emma realized she was falling out of character. "Do you?" she prodded.

"I train each day and..." He paused to glance over her shoulder. "I have a special diet."

"Ohhh." Emma rubbed her finger back and forward across his tanned upper arm. "It's working." *What special diet?* she wondered with a trace of frustration. Perhaps if she shook him, she'd rattle the answer loose faster. Flirting wasn't helping. "I'd like to muscle up. Is there a fast way to do it?"

"You'd need to train every day for a few hours." His gaze held clear doubt. "Protein shakes might help. And you'd have to diet."

"Diet?" Bloody cheek of the man.

He shrugged. "The changing rooms and showers are in there. Ladies to the left and men to the right. And that's about everything." He halted by a row of stationary bikes facing a large video screen.

People drifted into the gym in ones and twos. Emma was pleased to see there weren't many people in bright-colored spandex, the vision that popped into her head whenever she thought of a gym. Most people wore comfortable shorts and a T-shirt similar to her sleeveless top and stretchy back shorts.

Emma smiled brightly. "Okay. I'm interested. What do I do next?" She didn't intend to leave until she had answers.

"We do a fitness check. I can schedule one for you. I have a personal trainer session in five minutes, otherwise I'd offer to do the check for you now."

"Okay." Great. A fitness check. Emma hoped it didn't involve too much exertion. Her muscles were sore from the sexual gymnastics of the night before.

They walked over to the receptionist's desk, and Emma scanned the gym. There were five, no, six beefy young men wearing the resort's uniform. Not a scrawny specimen among them. Even the two women employees she saw bore impressive muscles but it might be a coincidence. Jeesh, how was she going to discover the truth? Perhaps they needed to check the premises during the middle of the night when no one was around. Maybe the offices and places that were off-limits to guests.

"Jamie can do a fitness test, but she'll be another five minutes since she's with a client."

"That's fine," Emma said.

"Come with me, and I'll show you where to wait."

Emma followed her guide through a narrow corridor she hadn't noticed earlier. They passed two offices then came to a third room. Her guide opened the door and gestured Emma inside.

There were charts on the wall with illustrations depicting people doing different warm-up exercises.

"See if you can follow the diagrams and do a few stretches while you're waiting for Jamie. She won't be long."

"Thanks for the tour." Emma smiled and fluttered her lashes, keeping up the image of witless to the end.

Her guide left, leaving the door slightly ajar. Emma debated if five minutes would be long enough to explore the offices next door and decided to risk detection. She was halfway out the door when she heard several masculine voices in the office close to where she stood. *Bother*. Emma dithered, wondering what to do.

Raucous laughter suddenly filled the air.

"The couple in room 243?"

Emma stiffened. Shit, were they under investigation? She edged out, flattening against the beige walls so she could eavesdrop.

"Oh, yeah," a loud voice said. "They rut like rabbits all night long."

Emma's mouth dropped open. Rabbits? Someone had heard them? How mortifying!

"What do they look like?"

"Both tall. The guy looks dangerous. Not the sort to meet in a blind alley on a dark night."

"What about his partner?"

"A bit big for my tastes."

"What are you talking about, dickhead? Her ass is fuckable," a third person said. "I'd ram one right up her anytime."

Emma's jaw sagged so much it was a wonder it didn't hit the ground. These men had not only heard them, they'd watched them as well. But how? Why? Emma groped for understanding.

"How's the take for this couple?"

"Through the bloody roof. We've earned more in three days than we made for the whole of last week."

People paid to watch her and Jack have sex? That was disgusting. Heat flooded her body followed closely by anger. Making love to Jack was private, dammit. Strictly because that was what Emma was doing—laying out her heart. The idea of other people watching...

"They're filming tonight and intend to release it as an amateur movie. It should win a prize for sure as well as make a ton of money."

Emma felt her face turn scarlet. Her teeth gritted so hard they were in danger of cracking. A tic burst into life in her jaw.

They were not going to get away with their home movies.

CHAPTER 6

Footsteps at the far end of the passage galvanized Emma to action. She whipped back inside, easing the door shut behind her. Oh, boy. She had to get a grip. Warming up. That was what she was meant to be doing.

Emma sprinted over to the closest poster on the wall, rapidly read the instructions and attempted to emulate them. The muscles at the back of her thigh groaned in protest, sending a wave of jagged pain the length of her leg. She winced and eased up on the stretch. Cripes, if she'd known sex with Jack would be so strenuous, she would've gone into training first.

"Though why you're worrying when Jack has told you there's not going to be any sex once we're off the island," she muttered. Thinking of sex brought her back to the main problem.

Movies.

Of her and Jack.

Naked.

The door flew open and a tall redhead stepped inside. "Oh, good. You're warming up already. Excellent."

Oh, she was warming up all right, and busy thinking of payback.

"You look as if you're ready. I'll weigh you, take some muscle-to-fat ratios then we'll test your existing level of fitness. But first, I'll get you to fill in this form with your medical history."

Emma stopped torturing her limbs and accepted the paper and pen from the woman.

Three quarters of an hour later, she teetered from the room on weak, rubbery legs. Jamie was a sadist.

She slowed as she passed the offices, but the men had gone so she had no way of identifying them. Though she'd recognize their slimy voices if she heard them again. That was for sure.

The thought of putting them in their place reinvigorated her and she picked up the pace from a teeter to a stomp. At reception, she stopped to learn the gym hours. A little recovery time wouldn't go astray. She'd come back later to do her first training session and ask more questions. Right now, she'd find Jack and let him know of her discovery.

Jack found her first. As she strode along the beach, a hand curled around her upper arm, jerking her to a stop. She whirled, ready to defend herself then relaxed. "Jack." She straightened, tossing her head as his dark glower hit her. At least, she assumed he was glaring because the line of his mouth was straight and firm. Difficult to confirm since he wore sunglasses.

"Where the hell have you been? I've been looking for you everywhere."

"I didn't know you cared," Emma said sweetly. No mistaking her tone for anything but snide and bitchy. Despite looking for him, he wasn't forgiven for blowing hot and cold. *Jeesh*, that sort of behavior was part of a woman's agenda. Men were supposed to be black and white, not shades of marbled gray.

"I was worried." He took a closer look at her face and had the effrontery to stroke a finger across her flushed cheek. "What's wrong?"

Emma jerked from his touch and stalked farther along the beach before dropping onto a clean patch of sand. With legs outstretched, she stared out to sea. She felt rather than saw Jack sit at her side. He could've put a shirt on, dammit.

"I've been at the gym. I wanted to follow up on something I heard from the bartender yesterday. While I was there, I overheard some men talking. Our room *is* bugged." She turned to Jack, feeling the full thrust of anger and indignation and loss of privacy sweep through her again. "They're filming us having sex. They're going to sell it on the internet."

The concern faded from Jack's face and he suddenly seemed more alert. Dangerous and in private investigator mode. She couldn't tell what he was thinking because of the glasses shielding his gaze. Bother the man and his rigid control. Just for once, she'd like to see him lose his cool.

"Aren't you going to say anything? Frankly, I'm pissed. What are we going to do about it?"

"We aren't going to do anything."

"What?" Her screech of outrage scared a foraging seagull. It took off into the air with a startled cry. "You knew? Why didn't you tell me?"

"I didn't think you'd be able to keep up the act if you knew we were under surveillance."

Right. This just kept getting better and better. "You could have given me the benefit of the doubt."

"I wasn't sure if they were onto us or not. It seemed better to ignore them and watch developments."

"And?" She didn't bother to hide her testiness.

Jack rolled toward Emma and tugged at a short springy curl just behind her ear. She was ready to blast him, but he spoke first. "Someone is watching us right now."

Jack scrutinized her as he fingered another curl. He'd never seen her in this mood before—curt, irritable. Plain bitchy. He liked it.

"What are you doing?"

"We're going to give another show for our audience. Let's see how your acting skills shape up." Her blue eyes narrowed, making him want to laugh. "I dare you."

She landed on top of him before he could blink, knocking the air from his lungs. Her leg slid between his, her thigh riding high against his groin. Instantly his cock lengthened, and he knew by the gleam in her eyes she recognized her effect on him.

"I was thinking of a kiss." But his body had other ideas.

"Well, what's stopping you? Don't say the audience is putting you off," she mocked.

Jack glanced up and down the beach. Empty, apart from the guy over on the far balcony. And he wouldn't see them either if they moved closer to the gnarled pohutukawa tree a few feet away. The sun streamed from directly overhead, and Jack didn't need to check his watch to confirm the time. Almost midday.

Cupping her face in his hands, he savored the buzz of his waking taniwha simmering beneath his skin. "Nothing stopping me at all."

He closed the distance between them so her breasts brushed his naked chest. Surprised she was even talking to him, let alone letting him get this close after this morning, Jack wasn't about to shrink from her challenge. He covered her lips and kissed her, really kissed her, thrusting his tongue deep into her mouth.

"Get a room, why doncha," a loud masculine voice hollered. He followed up his suggestion with a shrill whistle.

A feminine giggle joined his sniggers.

Where the hell had he come from? Jack lifted his head, his

gaze touching on Emma's lips. They were pink. Swollen. And he enjoyed caressing them more than he should. "Guess we'd better go to lunch. See if Mahoney has arrived back from the mainland. I heard the receptionist mention he'd left. He was away overnight."

"Have you found anything helpful?"

"Nothing. Just a gut feeling." Jack stroked his finger across her silky cheek. His instincts were working overtime, but he couldn't be sure if it was edginess because of the blue moon or intuition about the case.

"All the male employees are big. Muscled."

Difficult not to notice them, then there were the security guards who patrolled the perimeter of the resort. Keeping people in or out? Hard to say. "Did you notice the trophy cabinet at the gym?"

"Bulging with shiny trophies."

Jack rolled off her and climbed to his feet. He extended a hand and helped her stand. "I'm going to search the admin offices tonight."

"What time? How are we going to get around the watcher problem?"

"I'm not taking you with me." Jack didn't want to worry about her, but one look at her face told him she intended to argue. "We'll talk about it later."

They walked along the beach, heading toward the main resort area and the restaurants.

"What are you doing this afternoon? I'm going to do a hike

around the far boundary of the resort. I want to check out a couple of boats I saw this morning."

Emma nodded thoughtfully. "That would be a good way to get drugs either on or off the island. This is so frustrating. We haven't learned anything new. We don't know anything more than we did before we arrived."

"A lot of investigations go this way," Jack said. Fuck, she thought she was frustrated. Try being a taniwha with a blue moon on the horizon. His mind turned to sex. *One-track bloody thing*.

"I have a hair appointment. I thought I might be able to worm something out of the hairdresser or at least hear the gossip in the salon."

Jack glanced at her curly brown hair and shrugged. She couldn't get into much mischief at the hairdressers.

"Okay. I'll meet you on the beach near the pohutukawa tree at six to discuss how we're going to get around our voyeurs."

"Perhaps we could stage a fight." The twist of her lips mocked him. "It wouldn't be difficult shouting at you."

Jack grinned before sobering. He seemed to do that a lot lately. Smile. And usually, it was Emma-related.

"Don't laugh," she snapped. "I still haven't forgiven you for this morning. You should know that I'm big on revenge so watch your back. You never know when I might strike."

Jack stilled at the idea of Emma plotting revenge. A fight. His mind immediately darted to the part after the fight. The making up... Alarm bells tolled inside his head. Hell. Emma Montrose was wriggling into his head, and it was bloody uncomfortable with her wedged in there. Made him think—impossible things—involving a future.

They walked into the restaurant, and some of Emma's poker partners gestured them to join their table.

Emma waved back and hurried over, giving Jack no option but to follow. She'd changed since they'd arrived. She seemed more confident. More everything. Heads turned as she walked past. Jack intercepted an avid, hungry gaze eyeing Emma's arse. He speared him with a dark scowl, his taniwha growling approval when the guy hastily turned away to make a selection from the buffet.

"Is everyone having a good time?" the hostess purred into her microphone.

The diners roared back a resounding yes, and she beamed.

As Jack dropped into the seat at Emma's side, he noticed several of the resort hostesses trot onto the stage bearing boxes.

Without warning, his gut churned.

"We have several appropriate gifts for males and females. In this barrel, I have discs bearing the name of each guest. A roaring sound filled his head as she read off the first name. A couple at the table on the far side of the room sprang from their seats. Jack relaxed fractionally on hearing the second name. Not theirs.

"And finally," the hostess said. "Jack Sullivan and Emma Montrose."

Jack and Emma shared a telling glance, and it was obvious to him they were thinking the same thing. They were being set up, and if they were the focus of attention, they couldn't wander the resort at will.

Amidst much clapping and ribald shouts, he and Emma made their way up to the front to accept their prizes.

"What have you got?" one of Emma's new friends asked.

Almost afraid to look, Jack ripped away the pretty steel-gray bow and tore the black wrapping paper from the box. He lifted the lid to an array of sex toys, scowled, and replaced the lid.

"Toys," he said.

"Emma?" her friend asked, curiosity shimmering in her voice.

Emma glanced at Jack, her brows rising in a silent question. He shook his head. She tugged the tape from the pink parcel and peeked inside.

A soft gasp emerged, and Jack noticed she seemed a bit flushed.

"What is it?" Each of her friends leaned forward to peer inside.

"*Ohhh*," said one. "That's the newest model vibrator out. Wish I'd won that!"

"Why would she want a vibrator if she's got Jack?" another said.

Emma sneaked a look at Jack and found him staring at her. A flush ran the length of her body and crawled into her cheeks. But in truth, the vibrator wasn't such a bad prize to win. Once they finished this assignment, she might need it, because finding someone to fill Jack's position would prove difficult.

Half an hour later, Emma finished her lunch and checked her watch.

"I'd better go. My appointment is in ten minutes."

"I'll walk you out." Jack stood and picked up the box she'd been given as well as the one he'd won.

"Where are you two going? Are you off to try out your prizes?"

Emma smiled politely, but the same anger she'd experienced earlier in the gym clawed up her throat to choke her. They'd probably been set up so that they won—props—to enliven the movie that was being shot with them the star performers. She wondered what other prizes she and Jack would win during the rest of their stay.

They left the restaurant with neither speaking until they were ensured of privacy.

"We're being set up." Jack gestured at the boxes he carried with a jerk of his chin.

"That's obvious. Just what I wanted. My sex life plastered all over the internet."

"Don't worry. We'll get them."

"That's a promise," Emma snapped, still smarting each time she recalled the males she'd overheard in the gym. "We'll bust their asses for both drugs and illicit filming."

Jack grinned. "That's my girl." He leaned forward to kiss her square on the lips.

Emma's heart somersaulted. If he wasn't interested, why was

he kissing her? They didn't have an audience. *Men.* She sure as heck didn't understand them. Her lips softened under his, and she pressed into him even though the two boxes he carried dug into her ribs. Every breath she took was full of his scent. A groan built deep in her chest. Her pussy heated, moistening her panties. A perennial situation when she was around Jack. All she needed to do was think of him and her body prepared for his possession.

Their lips slid together. Sipping, nibbling, tasting. Mating. Her stomach swirled.

Jack pulled away with a curse, and they stared at each other for a long moment.

"I'll see you on the beach at six," he said. "Don't be late."

Jack paced the sand beneath the old pohutukawa tree and checked the skyline again. The last rays of sun brightened the horizon, but there was still no sign of Emma.

A couple paddled in the small waves that rushed to shore, slowly making their way toward the main part of the resort. It was a Middle Eastern night tonight so Jack presumed everyone was preparing for another night of frivolity—drinking, eating and dancing late into the night.

He paced away from the tree and shivered at his body's reaction to the pull of the moon. Even though it wasn't visible yet, edginess stalked him. He glanced down at his tented shorts with a wry twist of lips. Damn, he needed Emma.

The vibrations of approaching footsteps made him turn.

Emma.

Jack found himself smiling—an automatic reaction. He couldn't seem to stop.

His gaze scanned her from the top of her head, down her curvy form and long legs to her feet. Whoa! His gaze darted back to her hair.

"Hi," she called. Her body language screamed self-conscious, alerting him to the fact he could hurt her if he didn't say the right words. An opportunity to blow this budding relationship apart.

He didn't take it.

"I was starting to worry," he said instead.

She came to a stop right in front of him, so close they were almost touching. The back of his fingers drifted across her smooth cheek then he lifted his hand higher to tug lightly on a fragrant curl. It was the exact color of the sunset—a combination of red and golden brown and orange.

"You've got a sunset in your hair."

Her head jerked up, her blue eyes wide and uncertain at his compliment. "Is that good?"

"You look beautiful. Worth the wait." Jack hesitated awkwardly on hearing his words, but they came from the heart. And that gave him pause. What the hell was happening to him? This investigation was going nowhere. Frustration was his middle name, yet it wasn't the lack of progress that irritated the heck out of his life plan. It wasn't the impending blue moon.

It was Emma.

A sensible man who happened to also be a shape-shifting taniwha would do the job and walk away...

Jack shrugged and pushed away his insidious fears. Emma wasn't going to die because he was a taniwha. If he had his way, she'd never learn the truth.

"Discover anything helpful?" Emma sat on the sand and hugged her knees as she stared out to sea.

Jack dropped down beside her and cast a quick glance in her direction. "Nothing useful."

"Are you still going out tonight?"

"Yeah." Damn right. It was even more dangerous staying in their room.

"What do we do? Stuff the bed with pillows and make it look as if we're sleeping for a change?" She glanced over at him with an impish grin, one that made her resemble a mischievous pixie.

Jack stared. "It's so simple, it might work." He kept staring. Damn, she was pretty. He'd never noticed how creamy and touchable her skin appeared. His gaze drifted to linger on her mouth, and he found himself leaning toward her. Their lips collided and clung. A hand—Emma's hand—slid around his neck, urging him closer. They kissed until the need for air forced them to stop. Breathless, they drew apart.

"I didn't think we were doing that again." Emma toyed with the hair at his nape. Each sharp tug and scrape of her fingernails sent a corresponding jolt to his groin.

"We shouldn't be." But he gave in to the temptation to lick the delicate whorls of her ear. His mouth drifted lower to nuzzle and taste the soft skin of her neck. "But I was never big on rules."

"Me neither." She ran her fingers through his hair, still tugging hard enough to send a pleasurable pain to his cock and keep him in sensual thrall. "Are we going back to our room?"

They stared at each other for a long drawn-out moment. Jack considered everything he should do and immediately did the opposite. "Let's stay here."

Emma's mouth dropped. "Make love here?" She scanned the beach, glanced back at him and licked her lips. "What if someone sees us?"

"They're going to watch us if we return to our room." Just once, he wanted to love her without a paying audience. He pushed aside guilt as he scanned the high tideline. The situation was more complicated than a simple fuck. Uneasy, he shrugged and concentrated on Emma instead of emotions he didn't want to deal with. Besides, he'd hear the vibrations of footsteps coming in their direction long before anyone discovered them in a compromising position.

"That's true." She nodded, a slow grin spreading across her luscious lips. "I like the idea of cheating them out of takings and movie rights."

Hell, what had he done to deserve this woman as a partner? Once again, Jack shied from his thoughts. He'd fuck her since that was what they both wanted.

Jack pushed her gently back onto the sand. "Last chance," he whispered. "We don't have a blanket. We'll probably end up with sand in places that are uncomfortable."

"You trying to change my mind?" Emma's gurgle made him want to grin.

"Never," he breathed, placing a kiss on her fragrant cleavage. "Have I told you how much I like your tits?"

"Yeah?" Her face lit with laughter. "Why don't you show me?"

Jack scanned the beach again. The brilliant colors of the sunset had faded, leaving the horizon a dark, inky bluish-black. Overhead the pale moon shone, a day short of full.

His cock twitched insistently.

God, he needed her—it was that simple. He unzipped her shorts and tugged them down her legs. Purple panties today. Jack removed them, too, leaving her bare to his gaze. He parted her folds, sliding his fingers along her cleft, then Jack cupped her bottom with his hands and lifted her to his mouth.

Emma forgot they were out in public and concentrated on the feel of him. Her eyes closed, leaving her adrift in a world of senses. His fingers on her bare flesh, his tongue dragging across her sensitive clitoris. Heaven. The sensations built, lifting her higher until she shuddered, slow waves of ecstasy washing over her. With a final swirl of his tongue, she convulsed in a violent climax.

A soft kiss on her belly jerked her to full awareness. A grin spread across her face. "That was wonderful." An understatement.

"Yeah?" Jack checked the beach before ripping off his clothes. In the moonlight, he glowed, looking mysterious and magical. And so sexy, she couldn't believe he was with her. Even if it was just for this week. Emma chewed on the unpalatable thought. If she was persistent, she could win him over. *I'm going to make that man mine*, she thought as she watched him roll on a condom. Yeah, she'd win him over or die in the attempt.

Jack leaned over her, burrowing his hands under her shirt. "Are you brave enough to remove this?"

Emma thought for all of a second. "Take it off." Cool air brushed across her breasts, tightening her nipples to hard points. The contrast of warm and cold made her needy. Achy. Ready for Jack's possession.

He parted her legs and filled her with one seamless thrust. Pleasure grabbed her, and a cry escaped. Jack scored the tender skin along her throat teasing another soft cry free. He filled her, hitting the sweet spot, at exactly the right angle, sending her soaring. *Too quick. Way too quick*, she thought with a trace of regret as heat punched through her.

Jack thrust into her, almost impatient with his rapid strokes. A moan escaped him and deep shudders shook his large frame. His heart thundered, and she rejoiced in the fact she made him feel—something at least. She placed a tentative hand on his shoulder, only relaxing when he rolled off her and tugged her into an embrace.

Tears burned suddenly as she pressed her face against his chest. She loved him, but how the devil was she going to make him admit he returned the sentiment? Sighing, she cuddled closer just enjoying the moment.

They dressed slowly, laughing and snatching nibbles from bare skin before clothing settled back into place. Relaxed and limber, Emma was ready to take on anything. Jack reached out to ruffle her hair, the peacefulness on his face snaring another piece of her heart. She'd thought she'd known Jack, but each hour spent with him peeled away another layer of mystery. He was gentle and moody. Bossy and loyal. And she loved him even more than she had at the start of the week.

"I've been thinking about how to handle the search."

Disappointment surged briefly, but she shook it away and forced interest into her expression. At least he was sharing his plans, treating her more like a partner. If she couldn't have his heart, at least she'd have a working relationship. "How?"

Jack took her arm, and they wandered in the direction of their accommodation. He leaned close and murmured his plans. To anyone else he appeared as if he was whispering sweet nothings. Her heart lurched and used up so many beats she gasped and furtively massaged her chest. With his warm breath bathing her ear and his proximity she had to concentrate to make sense of his plan.

"We'll go back to our room. If our voyeurs are at their post already, we're screwed. If they're not, we'll stuff the bed with pillows so it looks as though I'm in bed."

"One problem with that," Emma said. "They must have some system of lighting. I mean we don't always make love with the lights on."

"I know. I've thought of that. The only thing I could think of was distraction."

Emma stopped walking. "A diversion?"

"Yeah. You and your vibrator."

"They'll film me!" She didn't have to pretend horror. It thumped her over the head like a sudden winter cyclone and left her anxious, her legs wobbly.

"Yes," he agreed. "The decision is yours."

Emma was still thinking about her vibrator when Jack unlocked their room and slipped inside.

"Wait there." It was an order.

Emma's breath came out in a hiss, his bossy nature going some way to shore up her bravery. He was impossible and as for expecting her to do a solo performance for the benefit of the camera... She waited for all of two seconds before darting after him.

"All clear," he said. "No one there yet."

"How do you know?"

"My hearing is excellent."

Was it her imagination or had his whole persona undergone a swift change? He looked awfully grumpy, and his dark eyes flashed with an emotion she had difficulty deciphering. Definitely not the time to argue.

"We'd better sort out the bed. I think there are extra pillows in the wardrobe." Emma jerked open the door as she spoke and grabbed two pillows plus a blanket. Jack tugged back the covers on the left-hand side of the bed.

"That's my side of the bed."

"It's farther from the two-way mirror." His mouth tightened. "Housekeeping has been busy while we've been out this afternoon. We have two cameras. There and there." He pointed before accepting the pillows from Emma.

Cameras.

Anger built inside until she resonated like a volcano ready to blow. They were not going to get away with this while she had breath in her body. One glance at Jack confirmed his fury.

"How are the cameras activated? Not by movement?" Emma glared in the direction Jack had indicated. She couldn't see obvious signs, but since he was an experienced operative, she believed him. "Are we being filmed now?"

"I don't think so. If movement activates the cameras, they'd film housekeeping and anyone who entered. They'd waste film. My guess is they record once they see action. They'd estimate from the timing of the dinners and special events which hours their guests would return to their rooms."

"But they must have had cameras all the time. That's what they implied when I heard them talking."

Jack scowled. "Going for different angles for their film, I'd say. But I think these are new. I haven't noticed them before."

A blush suffused her face. It seeped lower to heat her breasts. Surely, the way they made love wasn't that different. Not memorable enough to warrant more cameras.

Jack finished arranging the pillows and dragged the covers back into place. "How does that look?"

Emma tilted her head to study his handiwork. "Like two pillows and a blanket designed to resemble a person."

Jack's scowl grew darker. "Cut out the smart-ass remarks."

"I wasn't—"

"Showtime," he whispered. "I'd better go. Turn off the main light. Quick. Once I'm gone, you can turn on the bedside lamp on your side, but see if you can adjust the lamp so it shines away from the bed."

Emma nodded and followed him to the door. "Take care."

He grabbed her in a hug and squeezed her before kissing her hard. Then he slid out the door leaving her alone with the voyeurs.

Keep them busy.

The words echoed through her head—taunting and a touch repulsive. The idea of knowingly putting on a show for these creeps...

Taking a deep breath, she padded to the edge of the bed. After fumbling in the dark for a few minutes, she managed to swivel the bedside lamp so it pointed away from the bed. Before she switched it on, she allowed her gaze to run over the mirror. If she hadn't known, she would never have suspected.

Maybe if she switched on the television. She could bore them into leaving.

Emma strode over to the television, picked up the remote and settled back to channel surf.

Eek! Not that channel. She cringed at the naked bodies writhing on the screen and hurriedly changed channels. Her head dipped in a slow, disbelieving shake as she registered the mass of bodies on a round bed. She cocked her head to view from another angle. There were so many people; it was a wonder they didn't fall off.

The third channel change clued her in to the truth. The television was strictly R18 and geared to amorous couples. She wouldn't find distraction in a drama or a cheesy reality show.

Emma picked up her e-book reader and tried to concentrate on her most current purchase, a book called *Alien Encounter: Janaya*. She chuckled at the antics of a dog and two aliens who'd crashed on Earth, but on reaching chapter three the hero and heroine started having sex. She hit the off button. Perhaps reading wasn't the best distraction either.

The phone rang. Not Jack? Emma's heart pounded as she picked it up.

"It's Caroline, your resort hostess. Is there any way we can make your stay more enjoyable?"

How? she thought indignantly. *More cameras?* "Everything is wonderful," she said, not bothering to hold back on the irony.

"Have I called at a bad time?"

"I was about to go to bed."

"Oh! Say no more! I understand completely. Just give us a call if we can do anything to help you."

Emma slammed down the phone, fury and frustration making her restless. She stomped past the bed and stormed into the bathroom. Perhaps she'd take a shower to ease her tension.

Twenty minutes later, Emma stepped from the cubicle and grabbed a towel to blot the droplets of water from her skin. Someone thumped on the door and kept thumping. At first, Emma tried to ignore the summons then she realized the racket should wake a sleeping guest. It would seem odd if the pillows didn't react. She wrapped a towel around her nakedness and hurried to answer the door.

"Hello!" The girl's greeting was breezy and her smile bright enough for Emma to see she used a tooth-whitening agent. "You and your partner are the lucky recipients of a mystery prize." She gestured at her laden trolley.

Yeah right. Emma fought the need to scowl in her best Jack manner. The cynic in her suspected the voyeurs wanted action in the bedroom instead of the sound of running water and the scent of perfumed steam.

The girl picked up an apple-green bag and dropped several small bottles inside. "Here you go. Some massage oils and special lubrication. Oh, and these are great. Some nipple jewelry!" She thrust the bag at Emma then with a wave, tottered off pushing her trolley.

Emma clutched the bag and slammed the door shut. These people were unbelievable. All to get a stupid movie. Rage colored her cheeks as she tossed the bag on the dresser with all the other *prizes* she'd received during the week.

They were obviously going to keep bothering her, so, she'd give them a show.

Emma grabbed the pink box containing her vibrator. She pulled it from the protective wrapping and deftly loaded the batteries. *It would come with batteries provided.* The vibrator buzzed to life when she pushed a button.

Okay. What other props did she need for her show? After checking the towel was secure, she padded across to her box of toys. Scented massage oils with a hint of the Orient. Just the thing. Nipple jewelry. Maybe Jack would enjoy that later.

She sauntered over to her side of the bed and bent over,

pretending to kiss the head end of the roll of blankets. Then, she sucked in a deep breath. Showtime.

After settling on the corner of the bed nearest the mirror, she popped the lid off the bottle of oil. Not bad. She smoothed it across her arms, legs and upper chest. A pulse throbbed at her throat as she stood. With a casual shrug of her shoulders, she loosened the knot holding the towel in place and let it slither to the floor.

Emma pictured Jack and imagined it was his abrasive hands smoothing the scented oil on her breasts, his fingers plucking at her aching nipples. The heady scent of cinnamon and oranges filled the air as she applied oil on her legs and across her buttocks. With a languid move, she dribbled oil on her belly. Damn, that felt good.

Heat pooled between her legs as her slippery fingers dipped lower, through her clipped pubic hair, to smooth down bare pussy lips. Emma caught her bottom lip between her teeth to bite back a moan. The friction of her damp finger was exquisite. Damn, she was getting off on this. Did that make her sick? Her anger had receded, replaced by pure lust and enjoyment.

Pleasure flooded her pussy as her finger did another exquisitely slow pass. Her heart pounded. Too much. Too fast, she decided. But she couldn't help tracing an unhurried circle around her engorged clit before she squeezed more oil on her palm. Her breasts next, then she'd add the jewelry.

Emma stroked more of the fragrant oil across her breasts with light feathering touches. She tugged at her nipples again and satisfaction swamped her senses. After skimming the instructions, Emma fastened the loops at each end of the string of beads and chain around her nipples and tightened them to a point shy of pain.

A surge of fiery sensation jolted her and a groan escaped, clawing its way up her throat. Red and gold glass beads draped over the curves of her breasts once she finished, tiny bells tinkling with every jagged gulp of air. Her breasts rose and fell, the beads resettling, the bells singing a delicate tune, and when she tugged on the jewelry, she balanced between pleasure and pain. The sensation converged, jolting pleasure to her clit. It shimmered and backed away like a shy promise, a suggestion of what might come, and she froze, almost frightened to move.

God, she was so turned on, it wouldn't take much more than a nudge to push her over the edge.

The snick of the door drew her head up.

Jack.

Heck, what about the blankets? Distraction. Emma picked up the vibrator and switched on the power. Widening her stance, she ran the vibrator the length of her cleft. She was aware of soft sounds behind her but didn't dare look because of their watchers. Ripples streaked to life despite the situation, the tautness of the jewelry at her nipples intensifying the heat, the pleasure.

Suddenly, Jack was behind her, his bare chest hot against her back, his erection pressing insistently, nudging her buttocks. His arms snaked around her middle.

"You make me hot," he whispered. "God, I need to be inside you now."

"Yes." Emma set the humming vibrator aside and a swift glance at him told her he'd discovered something to help their investigation. The excitement, the satisfaction glowed in his dark eyes. She winked at him. "Yes, Jack. You make me so hot. Fuck me now."

Jack turned her and bent her over the bed. Gentle fingers probed her slick channel, filling her then retreating. Before she could protest, his cock filled the emptiness. Two hard strokes shoved her into orgasm. She shattered, her body shuddering with the force of her release. Jack climaxed a stroke later while her pussy still convulsed with blissful spasms.

He rested against her for an instant before pulling free and tugging Emma to her feet and into his arms. His mouth lowered over hers as he plundered, kissing her deeply, driving her desire higher and winding her tight as a spring. Her last thought as they fell onto the bed in a tangle of limbs and tinkling bells was that she could never ever get enough of Jack.

CHAPTER 7

E mma headed for the gym and ignored the perky voice on the speaker system, extolling the excitement of the clay pigeon shooting lessons for beginners and the tournament for those more experienced. Maybe she'd check that out later. With Jack's discoveries last night—a computer with shipment details—the case was on its way to a conclusion. Once they found physical evidence and tied a few loose ends, their partnership would terminate. Back to the way things were before. Pangs of regret pierced her feel-good mood. Not exactly the same way because now her memory contained visions of a naked Jack and how it felt when his cock surged inside her pussy.

A businessman strolled along the corridor in front of her. Dressed in his charcoal-gray suit, he stood out in the casual beach atmosphere of the resort.

Mahoney. *The creep.*

He yanked open the fire door at the end of the corridor, saw her and paused to hold the door.

"Thanks." She shaped her lips to a pleasant smile even though she'd prefer to spit at him.

A return grin—one that urged into smirk territory—curved his lips, an echo of amusement shining in his expression. "You're very welcome, my dear."

Emma bit back her gasp with difficulty and battled her urge to shift her countenance to an all-out glower. He recognized her face, and it wasn't a big leap to a conclusion. Making love with Jack was private, dammit. Fury lashed her and accusations bubbled out before she could think.

"Mr. Mahoney, I want the films back."

Amusement made him appear sly. Like the dog that had polished off the last of the cat's dinner, his smirk widened as his gaze drifted up and down her body. "I have no idea what you mean."

Emma shuddered, and it wasn't with the same awareness she experienced when Jack paid her attention. Mahoney made her feel dirty with his slimy interest, and his attitude poked her anger to a higher level.

"If you don't give me the films you've taken of me and Jack, I will go to the papers. I will tell every single guest at your resort that you're filming their private moments without their knowledge. I will warn them about you peddling their images on the internet for profit." Her chest rose and fell with the force of her fury.

"I don't know what you're talking about."

The clear enjoyment, the leer told her he knew and he'd seen the films. With his gel-slicked hair, his designer aftershave and suit, he appeared self-important. Emma's right fist curled and drew back ready to let rip. His face. His gut. She didn't care what she smacked—anything to prick his smug ego.

But no...violence wasn't professional.

"Fine," she snarled, after taking a deep, calming breath that was next to useless. "I will contact the police and see what they say." She marched past, but his hand shot out and fastened around her forearm with steel manacle force.

"I don't think so, my dear."

"I am not *your* dear." Only one man for her, and it wasn't this creep.

With his greater height and strength, Mahoney dragged her, forcing her to trot at his side along the corridor before knocking on a door with his free hand.

Emma fought every step of the way. "Let me go."

The door jerked open and Mahoney pushed her inside a storage room. Small brown boxes were stacked on a set of shelves while a desk and two chairs sat between the door and the shelves.

Emma squinted, trying to read the labels on the boxes. Ah! Her breath hissed out in triumph. Bingo. The very storage room they'd been searching for.

The hulk who'd opened the door stood to attention. "Problem, Mr. Mahoney?"

"Nothing we can't handle." Mahoney shoved Emma farther inside.

Emma was pleased to see her struggles had messed up his hair. She yanked from his touch, and this time he released her.

"Keep her here out of trouble. Get a rope. We'll tie her up."

Emma backed up rapidly. She lashed out with her feet, landed a kick, but it hurt her sandaled foot more than it bothered Mahoney. Tears stung her eyes but she kept kicking and biting until the two men forced her into a corner.

Chest heaving, she glared at them and considered her next move. "Sore nose?" she asked in a cool voice.

Mahoney's helper patted his beak with a folded white handkerchief. The cloth turned red, and smug satisfaction filled her. That would teach him to mess with her again. George, her boss, would've been proud. She made a come-get-me gesture with both hands.

"Stop mucking around. You won't get away," Mahoney said.

"Make me."

The door burst open, heralding the arrival of another employee. Emma shifted her attention and Beak man took the opportunity to grab her. Seconds later, they'd trussed her tight and she was ruing her rookie mistake.

"You can't keep me here," she screeched. Hopefully, someone would hear the din and investigate.

Mahoney scowled as he raked a hand through his disordered hair. "If the noise gets too bad, gag her." He glared at her before striding from the room, the *pop, pop, pop* of the clay pigeon guns punctuating his ire.

Emma stopped mid-shout, pleased she'd knocked the smirk off his face. Best she save the yelling for later when she really needed to attract attention.

The magnetic pull of the moon gave testiness a whole new meaning. Jack strode to their accommodation, hoping like hell Emma was there and could be tempted into a quickie. As he passed the crowd at the clay pigeon event, his stomach twisted, pain slicing with the brute force of a blunt knife. He weaved through the onlookers, his staggering blending with their intoxication. Thankfully, the staff seemed to have things under control. Way more than him.

Sex. God, please let Emma be there.

He hustled as best as he could. Never had his level of agony lifted to these heights. He needed to slam into her pussy in the worst way.

A glance at his hand showed the dark stems of his claws beneath his human fingernails. Another sharp cramp almost doubled him over. He fell inside the room and scanned it urgently.

Emma wasn't here.

Shit. He was gonna have to jerk-off to stave off both the pain and the taniwha. Along with the thought came a sliver of worry. He hadn't seen Emma since this morning.

Jack ripped off his clothes before a wave of torture struck. He crawled into the bathroom before pulling to his feet in front of the mirror. His face glinted with the pale gray of taniwha scales. His hands fisted around his cock and he noticed that too glinted a pearl gray color.

Emma.

He concentrated, visualizing her in his mind. Her ripe curves. Her mouth wrapped around his swollen shaft. Jack pumped his erection, stroking with hard, even strokes. Not enough to send him over the edge but sufficient to keep the taniwha at bay. He stretched the process out for as long as he could before applying more pressure to his tip. The pleasure bubbled over, escaping his restraint, and he came with a rush in his fisted hand. As he cleaned up, Emma filled his mind.

Where the hell was she? She'd said she intended to go to the gym. He'd go there first. If anything had happened to her, he'd never forgive himself.

The guards scarcely paid her any attention. There were two of them and they resembled their clones who worked in the gym. They argued about who would take their lunch break first. Evidently, it was chocolate penis day, as well as clay pigeon shooting day, and the chef's recipe for the truffle filling was worth fighting for the privilege.

"Toss a coin," one said, his brawny arms and shoulders almost bursting from his blue shirt.

"Heads," the second one called. He'd shaved his head and his scalp glowed in the artificial light. The coin glinted as it tumbled to the top of the desk. "Yes. Yes!"

Baldy left, jubilant in his victory and whistling.

"Bastard," Brawny muttered and clamped a pair of earphones over his ears.

Emma stared at him in disfavor. Why did he bother? She could hear his loud, discordant rock from where she was sitting. She continued to eye him while stealthily wriggling her hands and fingers in an attempt to loosen her bonds.

Half an hour passed, interspersed only by the pop and crack and cheers from the shooters and their audience. Baldy returned, brandishing a chocolate penis.

"There had better be some left," Brawny said in a testy tone and bolted out the door.

Emma continued to work toward freedom, her gaze on her minder. Baldy swiped his tongue across the tip of his chocolate cock and moaned, his eyes screwed shut in ecstasy as he savored his dessert treat.

Good grief. He was taking eating to a new level. She stared, not wanting to watch but mesmerized by his performance.

His groan was an animal grunt, and when he pulled the penis from his mouth, she saw he'd nibbled off the tip. A trickle of the filling dribbled from the corner of his mouth.

Eew. She shuddered and looked away. That was so *not* sexy.

Without warning the rope binding her hands loosened—just a fraction. Victorious, she doubled her efforts and five minutes later, one hand slid free. She drew her legs up in a stealthy fashion and unfastened the rope around her ankles.

What she needed now was a weapon.

Carefully, she scanned her surroundings. There was no way she could creep out, not with penis-sucking Baldy right near the door. But he was engrossed...

Her gaze lit on a large rock. A doorstop—something to prop open the entrance if they were bringing in or taking out new supplies. She glanced from the rock to the man's head. An excellent weapon—if she could grab it before Baldy discovered she'd freed herself.

He continued sucking on the penis. Her lips curled in distaste while she worked on freeing her other hand. Then she blinked in astonishment. Even better! Baldy was nodding off.

She scanned the walls, the furniture and contents. Perhaps she should look in one of the brown boxes? A snore erupted from Baldy and a chocolate-colored dribble ran from the corner of his mouth. Holding her breath, she tugged open the closest box. It was full of foil packs containing pills. Emma slipped one inside her shorts pocket. A snort sounded. She froze, but when she spun to check, he was still asleep.

With her pulse racing, she stood and glided smoothly forward to scoop up the rock. It was heavier than it looked. And in truth, she wasn't sure she could hit a sleeping Baldy over the head. As she edged closer, she saw dark chocolate smeared his cheek. That settled it—she couldn't hit a man who resembled a defenseless kid.

Emma took another two steps and reached for the door, still holding the rock. Her free hand closed around the brass handle and twisted. The door squeaked.

Baldy jerked awake. "What?"

Emma threw the rock at him and ripped open the door. Baldy cursed. She heard a crash but didn't stop to check the damage. Instead, she sped to the main corridor and paused to peek around the corner. Clear. She took off at a sprint in the opposite direction to the restaurant.

Jack.

She had to find Jack.

Jack scanned the bodies in the gym, alarm growing. Emma wasn't here. He couldn't smell the girly floral soap she used and he sure as hell couldn't see her. He'd already checked the clay pigeon shooting area, but none of her friends had seen her, and she wasn't one of those shooting.

He stalked through the restaurant, searching faces, his gut churning insistently the entire time. If anything had happened to her...

Pushing past the queue of party people at the buffet, he ignored the comments about rudeness. She had to be somewhere. Outside, he checked the bar and around the pool. Down on the beach. Worry creased his brow while the pull of the blue moon created havoc with his body, his control.

Every one of his bones ached as if he had a fever and sweat glued his shirt to his chest. He forced himself to stagger along the beach, to push past the pain that made him shiver and shake.

All he could think of was Emma. The way she smiled. The way she pressed him and ignored his bouts of surliness. The way she gave her all every time they made love.

A derisive snort escaped him. Somewhere along the line, Emma had crept into the empty spaces inside him. It was a damn uncomfortable sensation, but he'd come to enjoy her presence.

A flash of red caught his eye, and he hurried along the beach to intercept her. "Emma. Where the hell have you been?" A wave of pain doubled him over. Sex. Shit, now. Jack jerked her against his chest, shuddering at the feminine feel of her. Her sunset hair was ruffled and dirt coated one cheek. He lifted a trembling hand, battling nausea and acute stomach pangs to unbutton her shirt. A quickie to take the edge off, to stave the pain and halt the shift to taniwha. He fumbled, his nails well on the way to transformation.

"We have to go now." Emma fought for breath, her breasts heaving, her brow moist with sweat. She glanced over her shoulder. "What are you doing? Shit! They're coming. We've got to hide."

The scent of blood distracted him, and his nostrils flared. The coppery tang was coming from her. He seized her hands and saw her wrists were bloodied when she pushed against his chest.

"What happened?" Damn, his voice was changing. Desperation swelled along with pain. Sex. *Now.*

"Run." Emma grabbed his forearm. "They're after me."

A gunshot punctuated her words, sounding much like the clay pigeon shooters, but Emma took off like a startled gazelle. She sprinted across the sand toward the river mouth. Jack lumbered after her, trying to focus on moving one foot after the other. Waves of torment engulfed him, sharp and intense. His hands had turned. If the transformation progressed much further, he wouldn't be able to come back—not for twenty-four hours.

The soft sand changed to oozing mud. It sucked at his sandaled feet and slowed his progress. Fighting the aches and throbs of protesting muscles, Jack paused to rip off his shirt and yank off his leather sandals. Pearly scales already covered his chest, ranging over more skin with each gathering minute. He glanced at Emma as she darted between two mangrove trees. His brave and determined Emma. He hobbled after her, struggling past the grasping branches of the mangrove trees that gouged his limbs.

The pungent scent of the mud and the salty tang of the water called his dragon soul.

Emma.

Regret pierced him along with sorrow, and in that moment, he realized he cared more for her than he ever had for another woman. And he was going to lose her, if he didn't scare her to death first.

Jack's senses sharpened. The thudding of running feet following them continued, the harsh sound of the men's breathing a signal to hurry.

"Emma," he growled. "Into the water."

Her face whitened noticeably. "No, I can't swim."

But he could since taniwhas—the species he belonged to—were creatures of the water. "Climb on my back." He had to concentrate to force out the words.

Emma hesitated, but the crack of a firing gun—closer now and not of the clay pigeon variety—galvanized her to action.

Jack ripped off his remaining clothes and waded into the

water. "Come." His low, growly voice was barely recognizable. He glanced at Emma and winced.

"W-what is happening to you?" The clear shock on her face told him the transformation from man to taniwha had progressed enough to traumatize a human. His gut burned. His throat tightened with the need to rail at fate. No time to explain. Their pursuers were still crashing through the undergrowth, coming closer, closer, closer.

He grabbed Emma and tugged her resisting body into deeper water.

"No. No." She attempted to dig in her heels, panic lending her strength. The men's shouts sounded near as they searched for them amongst the mangroves.

Knowing he didn't have another option, he allowed the image of his dragon to form in his mind. Muscles and bones lengthened, his face changed, elongating to fit the sharp teeth and fangs that developed in his mouth. His nostrils changed shape, as did his eyes. A long tail formed, making him appear larger than his normal six foot two. His arms and legs changed into strong, webbed limbs suitable for swimming.

Fully shifted, the taniwha resembled a water beast, half dragon, half Loch Ness monster in appearance, capable of inflicting mortal wounds to enemies. He waded deeper into the water, and Emma started to cling instead of attempting to flee.

Jack filled his lungs with air and began to swim. He kept just below the surface instead of diving into the watery depths as he normally would if he was on his own. Emma needed to breathe but if he kept his body low, she wouldn't be too visible. He headed for the mainland, his heart heavy.

Once they arrived on the other side, things would change with Emma. Her hands gripped him, fingernails digging into his hide, but after her initial gasp, she hadn't uttered a word.

Shock, he thought. She'd fear him now, and he hated the idea. Too late, he realized he wanted her in his life. He shied from the word love, but it felt uncomfortably close to the emotion he swore he'd never let into his life again.

Surreal. She was shooting through the water on the back of a beast. And that beast was Jack.

George Taniwha Investigators and Security.

Emma's heart thumped erratically, her breath catching as the waves rushed over Jack's back and splashed her chest. She scrubbed the water from her face and coughed as she swallowed a mouthful. Despite her fear, exhilaration echoed her distress.

The taniwha part of the company name was real. She was riding on the back of a dragon. Jack was a taniwha. He'd shifted and grabbed her before escape entered her head. She wrinkled her nose.

Could be worse. She'd glimpsed his teeth. Children's storybooks hadn't exaggerated the sharp fangs.

Another wave slapped her in the face. An undignified screech emerged, and she wrapped her hands around Jack's neck. The water level crept higher. Reality check! She was in the middle of the bloody sea. God, she hated deep water.

Instinctively, she clung tighter, curling her fingers into the slippery flesh of the taniwha—Jack. Bands of panic clamped her chest, stealing her breath. She was gonna drown, and no one would ever learn of her fate. They'd go back to the island. Yes. *Great idea*. She glanced over her shoulder, and her shoulders slumped. The three men brandishing guns on the shoreline put a realistic spin on the situation. They didn't seem worried about the guests, although most were at lunch or at the clay pigeon shooting and wouldn't notice the danger in their midst.

No, returning wasn't an option.

She gripped Jack with her knees and kept her gaze off the endless expanse of water. How fast did a taniwha swim anyway? Faster than a boat?

Emma concentrated on the mainland, all the while praying they'd get there quick. She wondered about George and his sons. George's wife Meri. Were they all taniwha? Did they look like Jack?

The taniwha changed direction without warning, and Emma dug her fingers into the dragon's hide for greater purchase. Alarm almost choked her until she realized Jack was heading for a part of the coast covered in bush. The first thing she intended to do was get her feet on solid ground. She might even kiss the solid surface. The waves increased in size without warning.

Emma shrieked as one broke over her head. Panicked, she struggled, one hand loosening its grip on Jack to flail to the surface. Air. She needed air now.

A growl filled the air, vibrating through her ears in sharp warning. Then, her head cleared the water and she sucked in a hoarse breath. Another wave crashed to shore, but this one struck at shoulder level.

The taniwha swam then stood at the water's edge, four powerful limbs taking them to shore. Emma attempted to scramble off the creature's back, but Jack roared. She froze in place, unsure of what to do next.

Jack lumbered up the beach with her on his back. He was a pretty color—reminding her of the inside of a green-lipped mussel shell—pearly gray with hints of pink and green. The color was the one attractive thing about the dragon. Emma found it hard to believe Jack and the taniwha were one. Jack was a man to die for. The taniwha was...had a face only a mother could love, yet they inhabited the same being. Her mind stuttered, and the blip in her thought processes cleared.

They were the same, and she really, really liked Jack.

Problem solved.

They crashed through low scrub and bush until Emma couldn't

SHELLEY MUNRO

see or hear the sea. The secondary regrowth gave way to larger trees—punga, karaka, and manuka. The dragon continued with its uneven lope, taking a small overgrown path. Ferns brushed against them, and the leaf litter cracked under its feet, but Emma couldn't hear a single bird.

The taniwha—Jack—never hesitated. Gradually, the shadows gave way, and they emerged into a clearing. Jack stopped, and she cautiously pried her fingers free and slid across his slippery back to the ground. They eyed one another, but the taniwha broke contact first. He lumbered over to a punga and stripped several of the branches from the fern tree. After laying them on the ground, the taniwha turned to her and gestured with a clawed arm.

Okaay. It appeared they were staying.

"I'm going to find help." Emma turned to leave.

A roar echoed through the clearing. Strident like a clap of thunder directly overhead, the bark of sound made her leap in fright. She took another step, and the taniwha sidled closer and herded her back to the leafy bed on the ground.

"All right," she snapped. "I get the picture." Maybe there was something of Jack in the taniwha after all. They were both bossy.

Emma sat on a fallen log and glared. The dragon's mouth widened, and she could have sworn the creature was smirking.

Day passed to night, and the temperature dropped. Emma shivered, fighting the need to sleep, her head dropping to her chest before she jerked awake again.

Suddenly, Jack grunted. He ambled over and scooped her off the log before she could scramble away.

"I don't think—"

He growled and flashed his teeth.

"All right!"

Jack placed her on the fern bed and positioned himself beside her.

"You could have told me instead of scaring me half to death. I thought you were trying to drown me," Emma stated with a trace of defiance.

Jack grunted, the sound coming close to a bark of amusement.

Emma turned away. She wouldn't sleep—she knew it—but she might as well pretend.

The twitter of birds woke her at first light the next morning. She rolled over, away from the clammy warmth to see Jack, still in taniwha form, studying her warily.

"Morning," she mumbled, self-consciously finger combing her messy curls. "When do you change back? You do change back, right?"

Jack grunted. He seemed to do that a lot but she was no linguist. Each grunt sounded much the same.

He walked heavily toward a path the other side of the clearing then stopped to glance at Emma.

She sighed. "All right. I'm coming."

They walked for hours, navigating heavy bush, scrambling up

and down hills. By late afternoon, Emma was footsore, tired and desperately hungry. When they reached a clearing and a bubbling stream, she stopped, refusing to go a step farther without rest.

She glared at Jack, half expecting a thunderous protest, but he shrugged and strode into the stream, where he spent ten minutes splashing like a playful child. Then, he stepped from the water and stood before her. His skin glowed in the sunshine. He shimmered.

Emma blinked as the air around him shifted. The length of his jaw changed, becoming smaller before her eyes. "He's transforming," she whispered, amazement coloring her voice as his long tail disappeared.

Soon, all that remained of the taniwha was the whiff of fish and mangrove mud that lingered in the air.

Jack took a cautious step toward Emma. She hadn't behaved in the way he'd expected. She hadn't screamed, at least until she'd realized he intended to swim to the mainland. "Aren't you going to say anything?"

"You make a very ugly dragon."

Jack scowled. "There is nothing wrong with my taniwha appearance. I look the same as all the others."

A slow grinned danced across her face as she scanned him. "You're stark naked."

"That's it?"

"Um, I'm glad we didn't drown?"

That was it? Reaction buckled his knees, and Jack sank to the ground.

She closed the distance between them and crouched beside him. She placed her palm on his forehead and frowned. "Are you okay?"

"The last woman who saw me in taniwha form panicked. She fled the scene and was so traumatized she crashed her car into a tree. It was my fault she died."

"Oh, please," Emma scoffed. "How was it your fault? You made her drive? You made her crash?"

Bemusement filled Jack as her wide, bright smile bloomed. He opened his mouth and closed it again. Hope bloomed, and his cock rose in a silent demand. She looked damn sexy with that snooty, superior expression on her face.

"So what do we do now? Have we got enough to fry Mahoney's ass?"

"Don't you care that I change into a dragon when the moon is full?" He'd leave the explanation about sex for later. The issue was clouded enough already. No, he'd give her the worst now. "When the full moon approaches, I need sex several times a day to help me maintain human form."

"It doesn't have any bearing on our case," Emma said, but her cheeks flushed a bright red. "Can we get Mahoney for running the sports-drug racket and selling illicit movies? We have to do something. He's a creep. Besides, I don't want our images for sale on the net."

He didn't want that either. They'd get back every damn copy and destroy the master. But maybe he'd keep one for private viewing. "I love you," he said, his gut bucking with uncertainty.

"You do? About time!" Emma dropped to the ground at his side. She plucked at the white flowers of a manuka tree before looking up to flash him a blinding smile. "It took you long enough to work it out for yourself. The sex part is fine with me. I enjoy sex with you."

Was that it? Didn't women get off on this emotion stuff? He stared at Emma, willing her to tell him she loved him, too. She wasn't a casual girl. She must feel something for him. They hadn't had sex, dammit. They'd made love.

"So, are we going to charge Mahoney?" She dug deep inside her shorts pocket and pulled out a foil pack of pills. "I took this from the room where they held me."

Jack straightened in alarm. "What did they do to you?" She seemed all right, but he knew about hidden wounds.

"Tied me up." She shrugged. "I managed to get loose, and I threw a rock at the guy they left to look after me."

Shit, she'd even escaped by herself. Why did she need him around if she could rescue herself? "We have enough to make life difficult for Mahoney," he said finally.

"Good. Let's go."

"I need clothes."

Emma surveyed him with a long, leisurely gaze then bared her teeth in a wide grin of unholy delight. "Does this happen a lot? I mean, you look pretty without clothes, but doesn't it get a little cold?"

Jack reached over to stroke her cheek. "Not if I have a willing woman to keep me warm."

"I won't share." Her eyes narrowed in warning. "I expect you to concentrate on me. No other women."

"Other women?" Jack didn't mind admitting it—he was having trouble keeping up with her today. She wasn't reacting how he thought she should. In other words, she was confusing the hell out of him.

"We are getting married. Right?"

"You haven't told me you love me." Jack didn't have to pretend confusion. Marriage? With Emma? The idea didn't scare him as it would have a week ago. In fact, the more he thought about it, the better the notion sounded.

Marriage and Emma.

That would mean no one else could steal her away.

"You silly man." Emma's blue eyes were full of laughter and something else. Tenderness. Caring. Her expression made him hope for a future and maybe children. "Jack Sullivan, I have loved you for months. Haven't you noticed that women fall over themselves to go out with you? Why wouldn't I want you? Come on. If we don't hurry, we'll have to spend another night outdoors." She stood and held a hand out for him to take. "You need clothes."

"I have a friend who lives not far from here. He'll help us, and we can report to George."

"Great. I hope he has food." Emma couldn't believe Jack didn't know how she felt about him. He grasped her hand and tugged until she fell against his naked chest. His eyes glittered as he stared at her, and her heart thudded with sensual awareness. Oh, yeah. She loved him like crazy.

A taniwha.

It didn't matter. Living with a man who changed into a less than pretty dragon worked for her since the sex was great. Hot. Mind-blowing. Awesome. In fact, it made her hot just thinking about touching him. As she'd come to know him more her liking and respect had grown. She grinned as another thought occurred. Was that why George and the rest of his operatives appeared exhausted at certain times of the month?

"I love you, Jack." Emma pressed a chaste kiss to his lips.

He hugged her and deepened the kiss.

She smiled against his mouth, feeling so happy she wanted to cry. As far as twenty-fifth birthday presents went, winning Jack's love was a doozy. And now she'd caught the man, she did *not* intend to let him go. It might take him a while to get the idea, but she had patience enough for them both...

Would you like to learn what happens to Jack's friend, Hone? Does he find the love of his life? Learn more about **Blood Moon Dragon**, the next book in the *Dragon Investigators,* here: https://shelleymunro.com/books/blood-moon-dragon

About Author

USA Today bestselling author Shelley Munro lives in Auckland, the City of Sails, with her husband and a cheeky Jack Russell/mystery breed dog.

Typical New Zealanders, Shelley and her husband left home for their big OE soon after they married (translation of New Zealand speak - big overseas experience). A twelve-month-long adventure lengthened to six years of roaming the world. Enduring memories include being almost sat on by a mountain gorilla in Rwanda, lazing on white sandy beaches in India, whale watching in Alaska, searching for leprechauns in Ireland, and dealing with ghosts in an English pub.

While travel is still a big attraction, these days Shelley is most likely found in front of her computer following another love - that of writing stories of contemporary and paranormal romance and adventure. Other interests include watching rugby (strictly for research purposes), cycling, playing croquet and the ukelele, and curling up with an enjoyable book.

Visit Shelley at her Website

https://shelleymunro.com

Join Shelley's Newsletter

https://shelleymunro.com/newsletter

Also By Shelley

Dragon Investigators

Blue Moon Dragon

Blood Moon Dragon

Black Moon Dragon

Snow Moon Dragon

Middlemarch Shifters

My Scarlet Woman

My Younger Lover

My Peeping Tom

My Assassin

My Estranged Lover

My Feline Protector

My Determined Suitor

My Cat Burglar

My Stray Cat

My Second Chance

My Plan B

My Cat Nap
My Romantic Tangle
My Blue Lady
My Twin Trouble
My Precious Gift

Middlemarch Gathering

My Highland Mate
My Highland Fling
My Elusive Mate
My Valiant Princess
My Highland Wedding

www.ingramcontent.com/pod-product-compliance
Lightning Source LLC
Chambersburg PA
CBHW051921240626
47153CB00004B/1319